PRAISE FOR DEVIN MURPHY AND *TINY AMERICANS*

"In *Tiny Americans*, Devin Murphy skillfully weaves a series of vivid, unflinching vignettes into a complex portrait of a family struggling with alcoholism, abandonment, and anger. Each snapshot is an astute character study, exposing the desires and vulnerabilities of the family members as they fall apart from one another and forge new lives. Epic in scope, *Tiny Americans* is a poignant examination of the ties that bind a family, and how enduring those ties may be."

—Kathleen Barber, author of *Are You Sleeping*

"Devin Murphy is a writer who can do it all. With *Tiny Americans*, he gives us the Thurbers, some of the most complicated, most endearing, and most memorable characters I've ever read. The smallest details of their lives are vested, effortlessly, with enormous power and exquisite prose. I turned the pages, breathless, and yet the scope of the novel is nothing short of epic. When people say fiction is true, this is the kind of story they mean—wherever you are and whenever you read it, you'll see that *Tiny Americans* is the thing that you needed."

—Nicholas Mainieri, author of *The Infinite*

"Absorbing and affecting, Devin Murphy's *Tiny Americans* looks unflinchingly at a family's early unraveling and tracks how such sorrow reverberates over the years. But in moments large and small, we also glimpse the characters' great capacity for love and an aching hope for forgiveness and connection. A sweeping and powerful family novel."

—Bryn Chancellor, author of *Sycamore*

"Luminous, tender, and wise, *Tiny Americans* is a strikingly realistic evocation of what makes and unmakes and remakes a family."

—Emily Danforth, author of *The Miseducation of Cameron Post*

"An ambitious coming of age story. . . . Murphy's debut novel is a purposely limited view of war, as was *The Red Badge of Courage*, but strong characters and compelling narrative convey the impact well beyond one family. An impressive debut."

—*Kirkus Reviews* (starred review)

"A stellar account of wartime sacrifice, loss, and suspense. . . . Jacob's final salvation is satisfying and inspiring. As one character says, 'It's the incidents we can't control that make us who we are.'"

—*Publishers Weekly*

"Devin Murphy's fantastic debut novel *The Boat Runner* is a lot of things—thrilling, tragic, well-paced—but maybe most of all, timely. With prose reminiscent of Per Petterson, *The Boat Runner* is a book that asks its reader, When does a person stand up? When does a normal person take action? And how does a person resist against overwhelming power? *The Boat Runner* is a satisfying page-turner, sure, but it is also an allegory for our time, a reminder of world war not so long ago, when fishermen, factory owners, children, and mothers became reluctant heroes, standing bravely against a sudden and twisted evil."

—Nickolas Butler, internationally bestselling author of
Shotgun Lovesongs and *The Hearts of Men*

"Poignant . . . acts as a cautionary tale for our own times. . . . The young Dutch boy Jacob Koopman, together with his family, lives in the middle of a morality tale, in which doing the right thing is often obscured by the need to survive. Devin Murphy has given us a moving, powerful, and important work."

—Joseph Kertes, author of *The Afterlife of Stars* and *Gratitude*,
winner of the National Jewish Book Award for Fiction

ALSO BY DEVIN MURPHY

The Boat Runner

Tiny Americans

A Novel

Devin Murphy

HARPER PERENNIAL

NEW YORK • LONDON • TORONTO • SYDNEY • NEW DELHI • AUCKLAND

HARPER ● PERENNIAL

Portions of this novel have appeared in slightly different version in the journals *New Madrid*, *Confrontation*, the *Greensboro Review*, *Michigan Quarterly Review*, *Cimarron Review*, *Shenandoah*, *Hawaii Pacific Review*, the *Missouri Review*, *Toad Suck Review*, *Many Mountains Moving*, *South Dakota Review*, and the *Pinch*.

HarperCollins books may be purchased for educational, business, or sales promotional use. For information, please email the Special Markets Department at SPsales@harpercollins.com.

FIRST EDITION

Designed by Jen Overstreet

Library of Congress Cataloging-in-Publication Data has been applied for.

ISBN 978-0-06-285607-4 (pbk.)
ISBN 978-0-06-288624-8 (library edition)

19 20 21 22 23 LSC 10 9 8 7 6 5 4 3 2 1

For Hyat, Nora, and Jude

Tiny Americans

1

Jamie Thurber, 1978

In the fall of 1978, our father brought home a stack of books from the library on activities to do with us kids as an attempt to get himself sober. He had *Taking the Kids Outside*, *The Dangerous and Exciting Backyard*, old back issues of *Seventeen* and *Boys' Life* magazines, and Boy Scouts training manuals. I was thirteen and my two little brothers, Lewis and Connor, were ten and nine. Of course we didn't know it at the time, but from that point on, what he read the night before would be implemented the following morning as the day's activities, and for a year this became his new parenting style.

"Today we are going to find the heartbeat of a tree," he bellowed into our bedrooms on a Saturday morning in September. We were to dress and meet him on the front porch in fifteen minutes. Our father had traded with a truck driver fireworks from his shop for a contact microphone and headphones. He used to run his store like a pawnshop, trading goods that he'd bring home for himself or for us kids. We each took a turn wearing the headphones while he placed the microphone into the warped knothole of a hollow tree. "That's the heartbeat," he told us as the soft shivering sound snuck into our ears.

That calming sound momentarily soothed the coil of nerves that had gripped me since childhood, and that I could not seem to shake. By the third tree, my father was yelling at my brothers again—"Boys, quit your grab-assin'!"—and he handed me the microphone and tried to separate their wrestling match. "Come on. Sit and be patient like your sister," he told them, and pointed to me sitting at the base of a large elm. I hunched closer to the tree like a dutiful daughter and let the rhythmic crackling and distant gurgling noises seep into my bones.

"The noises come from grubs nibbling away at the wood," he said, but I was beyond his voice and was already convinced everything around me was alive.

From what I could tell, our father's amped-up efforts at parenting began after my parents started going on their Wednesday night "dates," which really meant marriage-counseling sessions in town. It was one of the only times they were consistently in close proximity. If they were both at home together chaos usually broke out.

"You're not even listening, Terrance. Just listen for once, will you," our mother yelled. "You were told to be a better listener."

"Well, I was also told to tell you when you are being impossible to love, remember that?" he yelled back.

Then they'd quickly lash out at each other, going for the seams to tear the other down or reverting to a silence that wouldn't break until our father became too agitated to sit still. Then he took us kids outside and gave us lists of things we needed to learn, as if he were trying to systematically force on us an interest in the world.

"You have to know the world you're in to know who you are in the world," he said. Then we moved on to learning a list of backyard bugs, which he was in a hurry to teach us, like something essential was on the line. This only made us anxious instead of satiating anything in him. We'd race one another to find millipedes, crickets, grasshoppers, and potato bugs, which I secretly envied for their ability to curl up in their instant armor.

That October, he woke us early and we spent a long weekend making a stone oven in our backyard out of used cinder blocks, red bricks, and clay we dug out of the river bank that bordered the far end of the cemetery. He never considered what it looked like to people driving by who saw us carrying industrial-strength black garbage bags laden with clay, and shovels slung over our shoulders as we crept out of the graveyard.

There was also our aborted attempt at a compost heap that flattened and spread out into a smelly brown splotch of eggshells, rinds, and earth in the far corner of the yard. We made jack-o'-lanterns and collected pine cones. Connor and Lewis chased the Canadian geese that populated the cemetery. They would get real close and run away when the birds raised their wings and hissed. We collected their feathers, which I dipped in ink and used to write out my homework. We did leaf and bark rubbings until we had imprints of almost everything in the woods on our thin white papers. I suspected this was all an attempt to keep us out of the house so our father wouldn't have to go back inside and be with our mother.

My mother had her own obsessions. She was an artist and kept her studio in town, where she could often be found working on her sculptures and paintings. The paintings rotating on our walls correlated to whatever period she was in. My brothers brought several boys from their school to our house to stand at the shrine of *Naked Women #17* during my mother's "live art" period when our walls were fleshed with life-size drawings of nude people that she framed herself.

Then there was her fascination with Indonesian shadow puppets. She painted a large series of them using dark pastel acrylics. The puppets were solid-white reliefs against prismatic-colored backgrounds. They looked like Nefertiti-esque skeletons frozen in terrifying pirouettes. She brought those puppet paintings home one at a time. My father, brothers, and I stood around the walls with her, looking at what she had hung, wondering if we were supposed to interpret some kind of meaning she could not express any other way.

The shadow puppet she brought home that fall was the brightest. The white outline of the puppet was more demonic than the rest, as if the dark, silent shadow at the center of our lives had been emboldened to dance. I positioned myself between my brothers when she unveiled it.

"This is one of your best yet!" my father said.

"I like the colors," Lewis said.

"Me too," echoed Connor.

"This feels wonderful," I said. I wasn't sure if I was talking about the painting itself or standing there with them all together, but my mother kneeled next to me and engulfed me in her arms.

"Thank you," she whispered soft and warm into my ear, perhaps realizing I would forever remember her embrace.

Despite these few happy moments my mother shared with my brothers and me, neither we nor her art were quite enough to keep her rooted in our world. Whatever sadness haunted her kept its firm grip on her ankles and would not relent. So she kept herself steady by drinking, and by afternoon the drinking gave a lovely brightness to her face. From far away she looked like a blushing girl. It was only when you were very close that you noticed the faint explosions of capillaries just under the skin.

Over the course of the day she became more animated. Her German accent waned by lunch, so her voice trickled like smooth honey-water. By sunset, she was back to her thick, bitten-off syllables. Then, late at night, when she woke us up, I tried to understand her, really understand her, but it was almost always too difficult.

That November, she rolled onto my brothers' beds cheering because the Buffalo Bills won their night game. From Connor's bed to Lewis's, she bounced and whooped, and I watched from the doorway as in their half sleep they got excited and joined her heathen celebration. But I never asked what they really thought once they were fully awake, and realized they had never seen her watch a football game, and that her cries of "We won. We won!" were nothing more than some mistimed attempt to connect with her sons.

The next day, our father waited for us at the bus stop after school, pacing around in anxious little circles with red-rimmed, bloodshot eyes.

"Come on, I want to show you something," he said, and loaded us into the back of his old 1964 four-door powder-blue Oldsmobile—a large, boxy land yacht with one of the floorboards in the back seat rusted away, which allowed my brothers and me to watch the road fly past beneath our feet.

"Don't put your feet in the hole!" he yelled.

Eventually my brothers learned to scoop up handfuls of gravel from the driveway before getting into the car. They dropped the pebbles through the hole and watched out the back window to see where they ricocheted.

He drove us to a pond south of town, on the outskirts of a horse farm. The trees along the road were posted with Private Property signs. He parked the car, and the three of us followed him into the autumn woods. There, he took a bucket and scooped it full of pond water so we could look at the life inside: pond skaters, dragonfly nymphs, pond snails, and whirling beetles.

"This is where the real life is out here," he sighed to us. He had a magnifying glass that we used to find and collect frog eggs. When he found some eggs, we scooped them into a mason jar, which we took home to watch as the eggs slowly cracked open and the tadpoles grew bulbous foreheads, hind- and then forelegs, until we had a handful of frogs that needed releasing into our local stream.

In the evenings, I eavesdropped on my parents when they attempted sitting together on the back porch. They talked about the firework shop, painting, and the philosophy books my father brought home from the Olean Public Library. My father loved those books. He thought they were near sacred, and I'd listen to him talk about them from my window until my parents' voices began to slur from their drinking. Then I'd listen for the call-and-response of their tiny mood swings and the endless surrenders they required of each other. I'd lurch into fitful sleep wishing I could stretch my arms out the window, down the side of the house, and rest a hand on each of their shoulders to calm them—to let them feel how much I loved them both.

It was after one of those heavy-drinking nights that turned into something heated, my mother came to find me in my sleep. She woke me by shaking my shoulders until I sat up and looked at her. It was one of the last moments where there wasn't anything truly wrong between us.

"Don't ever have children," she said, looking me squarely in the eye. "Promise me you won't ever have children."

She was sullen, her words piercing through my sleep, and I saw her standing in the center of my life like a glass sculpture— translucent blue and desperately fragile.

I wanted to yell at her but swallowed those feelings because I didn't know what hidden need was pulling at her to say those things. The trajectory of her day was always building upward to some manic excitement about one thing or another, always ending like some sort of fabulous Roman candle, flowing light for a few incendiary moments before leaving that phantom path in the dark where the tails of fire had been.

I could never fully piece together why my parents were the way they were. The facts were shadowy; my parents were shadowy; everything about our entire lives was blurry-eyed—her from Europe, him from Montana, both seeming just as far away. When

I was feeling brave I'd ask about their earlier lives. When I asked my mother how she and my dad came to be married, she told me that they dated for a while first.

"Mostly we were fooling around," she said. "Once, he came into my apartment, burst through the doors from outside, soaking wet from the rainstorm he'd marched through, and stood there with a giant smile on his face and stared at me like he was really happy with life and thrilled to find me standing there."

"I mean it was my apartment!" she said. "Who was he expecting to be there?"

"Then he said he wanted to dance with me and came toward me. I didn't want him touching me dripping wet like that, so I moved out of the way, took one step to the side, and the drunk fool goes crashing by me. Both of his hands smashed clean through the drywall in my hallway."

She said all this like people were always showing up at her place, falling-down-drunk with inarticulate confessions of love, and crashing through walls like a cartoon character.

Because I never knew when my brothers were going to charge in, or when our father was going to call for me to explore the neighborhood, or when our mother was going to sneak in for one of her midnight sermons, I didn't trust the privacy of my own bedroom. So I got into the habit of dressing warm and sneaking across the street at night to the cemetery to give myself what Charlie Rutkowski from school called "the old sticky finger."

I went when it was late and would lean against one of the larger headstones set back from the road. I unbuttoned my jeans, and began rubbing myself until it felt like my body was lifting upward and floating.

In October, my father was hired to clear and remove the wood from a new property development near Chautauqua Lake, which he did with a backhoe, chain saws, and a rented flatbed semi-trailer with an attached crane. He brought the big semi loaded with logs down through town and let a big blast of the truck's horn go several times in succession in front of our house. I heard the horn and went running out.

On the street my father was in the big rig, the cab purring and lurching off the pavement. A drift of black smoke rising out of the chrome exhaust pipe, the disk lid popping up and down like a Pac-Man mouth belching fumes.

"Get your brothers and hop in," he yelled.

He drove us through the south towns. On the empty country roads, he let us yank on the cord that made the horn blare, and that was how we made our entrance onto a large Amish settle-ment with horse-drawn buggies, large red barns, and fields with mounds of cut hay spread out like bedded animals. We paid no respect to the quiet of the countryside that belonged to the men with untrimmed beards hanging flat off their chins and the women in denim-colored dresses with white bonnets, who stopped and watched as we went screaming by. Thick children with broad, squared shoulders covered their ears, and I waved to them.

"Thatta girl," my father said, but kept looking out the window.

I secretly watched his face as he drove, trying to decipher what he was thinking—how he felt about me at that moment.

At the center of the village there was an old sawmill where the Amish used draft horses and large levies hung from the barn to unload the felled trees.

"Let's go have a look," my father said, and led us to a kennel around the back of the barn. Dozens of large black Newfoundland dogs were separated by chain-link fencing. They were all giant to begin with, and each dog was also pregnant. Some had dark nipples hanging off their stomach like plump raisins.

"What is all this?" I asked.

"Where do you think those puppies at the pet store come from?"

"Can we have one?" Connor asked.

"Do you really want a pregnant dog?" my father asked.

"Well. Any dog," Lewis said.

"No. These will get goofier and goofier the more they breed them."

His answer didn't surprise me. We had avoided pets since Lewis brought home his kindergarten class's hamster over a school break and it clamped onto his tiny finger. He thought the animal was going to eat its way up to his knuckle. He slammed the clinging hamster against the paisley wallpaper as he ran from room to room, leaving blood splats until Mom finally dragged him into the bathroom, held his hand under the tap, and drowned the hamster.

The smell of freshly cut hay and dog urine hung in the air. The calls of men guiding the horses and the logs came from the back side of the barn.

When the logs were all unloaded my father handed the men

who did the work a list of furniture he wanted built from the wood.

"I give them the wood. They make the furniture, and in return they keep the leftover lumber. Then I'll sell the furniture at the store or back to whoever owns that big damn house being built," he said.

Early that December, my father took us for a scavenger hunt at the dead-car junkyard. On the drive across town he stopped into a local bar called the Tavern, and we all went inside with him. The floors were linoleum, and my school shoes glided over them until they got stuck on something sticky. My chin barely cleared the padded leather saucer seats propped up on chrome poles bolted into the ground. No sunlight made it into that room, and the man behind the bar, a scrawny guy who had an overwashed red flannel shirt and a cigarette-ash-colored beard, looked like he'd never seen the sun in his life. Behind the bar was a fat boy Lewis's age, named Lenwood Murry. He stopped washing the dishes, smiled, and waved at Lewis and Connor.

"Jesus," the bearded man said to my father, pointing at the three of us sharp on his heels.

"Don't worry. We're just passing through." My father pulled out a wad of cash from his wallet and slapped it onto the bar with his open palm. "This makes us square," he said, then he had us all turn around and walk out the front door, into the sunlight that stung my eyes.

"What was that all about?" I screwed up the courage to ask him.

That's when he reached down and gently wrapped his fingers around my neck and pretended to throttle me. My skin prickled at his winsome touch. "Look who's turning into Miss Nosey," he said, pecking my forehead before letting me go.

That same month we took a five-gallon work bucket out into the cemetery, toward the back part of the burial grounds. Our father had us make plaster casts of the animal tracks we had found. I filled a hoof indent a deer had made in the mud, Connor filled one that looked like it came from a small dog, and Lewis came back wearing one shoe and smiling with a plaster mold of his own left foot.

Our father put those plaster molds on our kitchen counter, where they shifted across the linoleum from one spot to another for weeks until he knocked them all to the floor while rooting around in the cupboard. He finally found a clear unmarked bottle that he held up and swirled in front of the light. He was frantic, and his forehead was dabbled in beads of sweat. The dark yellow liquid inside looked like pond scum. Then he shut his eyes and drank it all in one tilt without noticing me in the room.

As I watched him I could already see myself sweeping the plaster shards into a dustpan. Then I'd keep cleaning. All the deepest cupboards and closets. I felt a desperate need for him to pick me up the way he did when I was little, with one of those huge hugs where he spun through the room with me in his arms.

When he slammed the bottle down on the counter, he grunted and swung around like a giant animal. He froze and his hazel eyes widened on me as I watched the redness flush his face.

"Jamie!" he said.

I wanted to break all his fingers so he wouldn't be able to hold a bottle. I didn't want to stop there either. I imagined my mother's fine fingers in my hand as well, bending them back until the bones crunched and her own bottle dropped, and that image settled onto my brain like an itchy scab.

Late that December through January, during a stretch of heavy snowfall, my parents avoided each other entirely. Our mother spent almost the entire month at her studio and, since his relapse, our father became even more regimented with his daily tasks for us. He had us excavate and build elaborate snow dens that we packed into solid ice by dumping buckets of water on top. He cleared the snow in the backyard, laid down a couple of blue tarps, and set large boards on their sides to form an enclosed rectangle that he flooded to make us an ice rink. My brothers hip-checked each other off the ice into the surrounding snow. Once, Lewis sent me flying into a snowbank. Before I could get up, I remember my father lifting me to my feet and wiping the snow off me.

"I'm sorry about that," he said. Then he bent down and hugged me for a long time. "I'm sorry."

As he hugged me I felt as safe as I ever had.

The next day, our father tied a toboggan to the back of his Oldsmobile and dragged the three of us behind the car through the cemetery's iced-over gravel roads. My brothers and I held on to the person in front of us as we flew over the ice and snow, occasionally felt the grip around our waist loosen, and then let go, looking back to see whomever it was tumble out of view, a white rooster tail kicking up in our wake.

"Today we do birds!" our father said in late February, a library copy of *Birds of North America* in his hands.

Struggling through a deep hangover from another lapse, he marched us through the cemetery, hunting for the lift and twitch of purple martins and listening to the foreign language of birdsongs that floated on the air.

Then he wanted us to feed the birds in our backyard, so we built birdfeeders in our garage.

"I don't like doing this wood stuff," I complained while sawing a flat board along the lines he etched with a pencil for me to follow.

"Well, you're going to learn it anyway. That way you won't have to depend on anyone else to do it for you."

At the height of our production we had eight birdfeeders mounted along our backyard's fence. There were ruby-throated hummingbirds, starlings, sparrows, goldfinches, jays, and a few birds of prey ranging over from the creek and tall cemetery evergreens to our yard. The birds flitted from the feeders to our mother's intricate sculptures on the lawn. One of those sculptures had three twelve-foot strips of curved iron secured on a pivot that kept them moving like waves.

Toward the end of winter, my father scattered fresh acorn squash and pumpkin seeds out for cardinals, and when those ran out there was always a fresh spray of store-bought seeds and sunflower hearts sprinkled on the new snowfall. After heavy snows we had to clean the feeders so the seed wouldn't rot. We scooped out the wet and fetid pulp with our hands.

"You have to do this all the time. The birds are depending on you once you start feeding them," our father told us. His words echoed in my head when I went out early one morning into a light snowfall. I'm not sure if I heard him or sensed him nearby, but when I turned back to the house I saw him up on the top deck. He was standing there naked and looking out at the cemetery. He didn't see me, and I immediately moved back to the house in a quiet panic so as not to disturb whatever it was he was doing—watching over the birdhouses, hiding from our mother, or waiting for the cold to truly, finally wake him.

In March, our father decided to make a woodpile in the backyard and started splitting logs in an attempt to get back in shape. He took up jogging and jumping rope and stuck with those for a few weeks until the snow melted and he tired of both. Then he started having a few glasses of red wine with dinner because "it's good for your health," he said. Then he started buying the wine in gallon jugs and boxes with aluminum pouches stuffed inside that would deflate as he siphoned them down. Soon, the woodpile diminished, and he spent the time he'd been working out sitting at the kitchen table listening to a police scanner that a trucker who stopped by his store had sold to him. He sat for hours raptly tuned in to the garbled calamity of other people's lives.

By the middle of March, there had been a lull in his ventures to the library to get new books on how to entertain us, and he rarely left his radio chair if he wasn't at work. When we got home from school, he looked at us as if he were overwhelmed by our presence.

"Each of you go find me a spider in the house," he said, like he'd spent all day behind the counter of the shop thinking this up, as if idle time were the worst thing we could have on our hands.

"Why do we have to do this?" Lewis asked.

"So you'll know where they're at," our father said. He placed his open palm on the band of sunlight filtering into the room. Every inch of his calloused palm and fingers shone. Then he snapped his fingers into a fist. "Got it," he said. "The light. I got it. It's for you." He lifted his hand over Lewis and pressed it onto his head. "Now you have it. Now you're full of light to go into the dark and hunt spiders."

"I don't want to do that," Connor said.

"Well. Want in one hand and shit in the other, and see which one gets full first. Now go on."

That April my father tried to rally and finally did go back to the library for more books. We tried simple things, like going into the backyard and walking in the cemetery at night to watch the stars. We timed thunder and lightning to track a storm's encroachment. We went looking for mad March hares, and saw how they stood on their hind legs and boxed each other in the early morning. He woke us up once to watch the sunrise and came to us again to watch the sunset that night. "That's all the time you get in a day, to do what you want with your life," he said. "Did you use it to the best of your ability?"

On our way home, we cut the stems of pussy willows, which Connor called "fuzzy berries" and swung in front of him as he walked as if he were blind.

"They're the first life of spring," our father told us. "They need to appear before everything else because their pollen is carried by the wind and if they bloomed later, the full spring foliage would block the spread of the seeds. Do you see? It all makes sense."

Late one night in mid-May, we were driving with our father. My brothers were in the back seat dropping pebbles through the floorboard. From the passenger seat, I couldn't see over the dashboard when we hit what our father described as a red flash. He got out and stood behind the Oldsmobile. The headlights were still on, but we couldn't see what he was looking at. Then he bent down and picked something up, and when he got back into the car he said, "Look at this." He sat back down and lowered a dead fox into my lap by its tail.

The fox molded against my legs. Its eyes were open, and its tongue hung out against my jeans. It took my everything not to scream, and I shut my eyes and felt my brothers' hot breath as they leaned over my shoulders for a better look.

"She's beautiful," our father said.

The lower half of its muzzle was covered in a pure white fur that flowed down its throat and widened at the chest. The tips of its ears and tail, and all four legs, were glossy black, and the rest of it, from the crown of the head until the tail turned black, was a soft orange. The car filled with an overwhelming musk smell, and when I touched it there was a slick residue of filth on it.

"I'll show you guys how to mount it in the morning," he said, and put the fox in the freezer when we got home.

"We're not the kind of people who keep unskinned animals in our refrigerator," my mother screamed from the kitchen. She woke us all up that night when she got home from her studio. Her voice was heavy and mean, and made me spend the rest of the night wondering just what kind of people we were.

In the morning the frozen foods were still pushed to both sides of the freezer, but the fox was gone.

During a late May storm, it was raining so hard we were all inside together, and my brothers got each other so whipped up wrestling that they broke a lamp.

"What does it feel like right before you have a nervous breakdown? This has to be it; this is the feeling. You kids are driving me nuts," our mother shouted, lifting her body off the couch, and shuffling us toward the foyer door. "Put those jackets on, all of you, jackets on and outside with yourselves. Get out. Go play in the yard," she was pointing to our eight birdfeeders in the rain.

"It's coming down pretty bad," our father said. He'd been reading a library book about St. Augustine at the kitchen table and listening to the police scanner.

"Shut up, Terrance," she snapped at him. Then she turned back to us. "Go and stand out there for a bit and soak it all in."

The torrential rain was erupting the already-standing puddles in the grass, and as soon as we were in the middle of the yard our clothes were soaked through and slapped tight to our skin. The rain on our heads sounded like the magnified and pulsing heartbeats of a forest.

"A bunch of wet puppies," she said as she shut the door.

The three of us stood there looking accusingly at one another through the veil of rain, then at the closed door of our home, with the sad, sunken figure of our father watching us from the big picture window in the living room, and our mother looking out from the small window above the kitchen sink, where a waterfall over the windowpane blurred her face.

"Today is flowers," I can still hear our father yelling to us the next morning before we went out to find forget-me-nots, Queen Anne's lace, and goldenrod. My brothers made weapons out of sticks and pegged each other with rocks and crab apples. Later they sought me out to show me what they had found while I was collecting caterpillars. Connor held a jar forward with a perfect leaf-green praying mantis perched on a twig and spun it in front of my nose to admire how precise a creature it was.

When my brothers tired of the mantis, I took the mason jar to the back steps of our house and studied it before opening the jar and letting it go.

"Tonight you are to become bat detectives," our father said one June evening, handing us each a flashlight before he made us spend the night in a tent in our backyard, where the only sounds we heard were our parents hollering at each other.

"Be completely honest, and tell me—" our father screamed like there was an ax cleaving in half everything that was holding him together. Now I understand that his world was unraveling, that his marriage offered him no steady footholds and the natural world was the one place he felt centered, whole. In that year during which we had felt the strength of the rain, charted the sun's course across a clear sky, and dug our naked fingers into the numbing snow, he had been trying to show us a path to seek refuge and a different language that might heal us, save us.

"Tell me—" our father screamed again.

I didn't hear our mother's answer, so I didn't get the context of what they were fighting about. I tried to distract my brothers and lull them to sleep by pretending we really were outside to sleep beneath what we were told would be "a healthy swarm of bats." But they knew better; we had been pushed away from my parents for years because of such fights. Fights that ripped us clean of our flesh and left only raw notes of nerve ends, such that we could not bear looking at one another any longer. Our vulnerability was too painful to see.

The next night, I stayed in the garage studio and my brothers opted to sleep outside again. And the night after that, too. For a week my brothers didn't come back into the house. Together in that darkness, they must have finally caught up to me and what I already realized—that our parents were to be counted among the alcoholics, the toxin-fueled, the lost. This one secret of the world, we knew.

2

Connor Thurber, 1984

We grew up within biking distance of the city park in Olean, which sits in Western New York's Southern Tier, at the crossroads of the Rust Belt and the northernmost foothills of Appalachia—me; my older brother, Lewis; our sister, Jamie; Lance and Brian Borgowitz (twins); Levi Smith; Jack Vander-Camp; Jessie Roberts; Samuel Bergman . . . a whole slew of us. The park had basketball courts with these tectonic cracks that made the surface too uneven to play on, a baseball diamond with crab apple–size stones littering the infield, and a wide strip of tall conifer trees that walled off a quarter-mile gravel track. The field inside the track is where we would play football.

We were a bunch of white kids with mostly immigrant names. Our grandparents or great-grandparents moved here to work the steel mills, bought houses, and had families until Lackawanna Steel faded in the late fifties. In the early eighties, what was left for us was the strip mall on State Street with a full regiment of military recruitment offices. Our grandfathers,

fathers, and older brothers had signed their names to contracts, and we knew we, too, would end up sniffing around those doors once we turned seventeen. There was no talk of not joining the military—only of which branch.

A lot of us had fathers and older brothers who had gone into an army that had either taken them away for good or delivered them back to the same spot coiled too tight for domestic life. They took jobs with the sanitation department, worked the third shifts at the Cutco or Zippo factories, ran firework shops, or were long-haul truckers we rarely saw. Some moved west for better jobs. We wore their moth-eaten Buffalo Bills gear, pulled from boxes in basements and attics, their names etched on the flaps in the looping black letters of our mothers' handwriting.

Playing football in their old sneakers and cleats stripped us of all our insecurities. We were beaten free of timidity and varnished in deep-muscle bruises. Getting hurt was our continuous initiation. There was the frump of air knocked out of our chests, nut shots, concussions, chipped teeth, the red specks of blood on the wet scabs, and skin torn open like split grapes so we could see the mystery of our stewed-tomato insides. We thought our fathers would be proud of how tough we were becoming.

That field and those games became our collective fallout shelter to hide from our home lives. We each tried our best to silently smash our worries away, leave them turned up in clumps of mud we scarred the grass with. And though nothing was ever so clear, our mere presence day after day was our unspoken attempt at saving one another.

With the exception of the annual circus that came through town, the only time the park was not ours for the taking was in the fall for the high school's homecoming party. The fire department would spend a whole day making a house-size mountain of wooden pallets. Then they'd drive two trucks onto the grass and park on both sides of the woodpile. That night, as it got dark, everyone from the high school would come to the park. The firemen were in charge of soaking the wood with five-gallon red plastic drums of gasoline. They'd let an alumni, a half-mad giant Vietnam vet named Tiny, light the fire in his 1960s school sweater, and he'd go around the outer edges of the wood and light wadded-up tips of newspapers to set the wood aflame.

The only fire we'd ever seen that was larger came from Charlie Rutkowski's family-owned gas station that blew up on a January evening and sent an incendiary cloud of smoke about a mile into the sky. Mr. Rutkowski was dejected even though his insurance paid him off what Charlie called "a shit ton of money." Charlie Sr. didn't get another job and sold the land to a Dunkin' Donuts franchise. He spent the rest of his life either mowing the lawn once a day, or shoveling in the winter, slow scoop by slow scoop, as if he was hoping time would hurry up and dismiss him from something.

Lewis and I liked fireworks, liked setting them off. Lewis supplied the whistlers. When our father's firework shop shut down and he moved out west, the supplies were put into a storage unit with his books and forgotten about by everyone but Lewis. On weekend nights, Lewis and I and our friends roamed around in small packs, forming and re-forming at the park. Lewis divvied up what fireworks he brought, and everyone took their lighters and scattered. You could see in the darkness little flickers of Zippos or match tips breathing orange for a moment, then the screaming trail of sparks shooting off into the night. I did my best to aim them at whomever I thought I could hit. Most whistlers would take some schizophrenic path through the air and fade out somewhere over the baseball diamond. Direct hits would smack the skin like a wasp sting and leave welts. Both Lance Borgowitz and Charlie Rutkowski had whistlers fuse to their shirts and burn holes the size of volleyballs in the cotton. Most of us had a whistler brush by our heads at least, which was part of the manic fun. Being close to something scary that we could feel on our skin.

Lance Borgowitz's father was in prison for murder. That left Lance and his twin brother, Brian, alone with their mother, who couldn't control them. The roof of their ranch-style house was warped from the weight of year after year of snow. Where the roof dipped to the ground over their living room window it was propped up with long four-by-fours dug into the dirt. We joked how their house would tumble down when the Borgowitz boys threw each other through the supports. When that actually happened, we teased Lance and Brian about the slide of rubble slipping out of their bedroom wall to the front yard like a spiky tongue.

Jason McKillroy had a skin-pigment issue. He had bleached white and brown blotches of skin that pixilated where the blotches met like swaths of freckles. Jason was easy to like, but you could never keep your eyes from running over his face and seeing how the lobe of his left ear was a tanned-leather brown and the lobe of his right was sugar white. When we played shirts and skins, there was the momentary silence as he revealed his Holsteinesque torso, and we'd all told or heard the jokes speculating about the odd hide of his penis.

Football was everything to us then. One night after one of our games, we went to Samuel Bergman's trailer to watch the Bills, who had lost all ten games so far that year. When we got there, Samuel's mom wouldn't let any of us in and told us all to go home because we were filthy. She didn't even want Samuel to come inside. I remember the look on his face, like he'd hated her for everything that ever hurt in the world. We all walked to his backyard and hunkered under the trailer's back deck. The wet snow dripped through the wooden boards and fell on us where we sat in the cold dirt. Samuel snuck in the back door and ran an extension cord and radio out so we could at least listen. The game had started by the time he turned the radio on and the announcer was screaming, "Greg Bell to the *twenty*! To the *fifteen—ten— five—touchdown*!" and we all joined in and screamed, "Let's go, Buffalo! Let's go, Buffalo," like we were some wild and beautiful family, cracking our elated fists against the underside of the deck.

Samuel's mother came out, and before she could say anything from the doorway, Samuel started screaming at her from under the deck, "We're not in the goddamn house, so leave us alone—leave us alone—leave us alone!"

His mother stood there for a moment before she went back inside, leaving us in the mud, the cold making us shiver.

Our beloved Buffalo Bills. Each of us knew as much about that team as the friends we were huddled up under the deck with. We had cheered for their players, Darryl Talley, Joe Ferguson,

Greg Bell, Byron Franklin, Jim Haslett, and prayed they'd win just one game for us. We knew everything about them. Samuel was the only one among us who had ever been to the stadium to see a game. His father had taken him three years before. He described the whole crowd standing with everyone leaning over the seats in front of them so it looked like the entire place was swallowing itself from the upper decks inward.

The Bills' legendary lineman Fred Smerlas allegedly used to chew worms during games to gross out his opponents. My classmate Peter Verdino tried it and stuck a night crawler in his mouth during a huddle, but vomited on his shirt before he made it to the line of scrimmage and had to sit out the rest of the game because no one wanted to touch him.

Levi Smith was another guy in our group. He would fight anyone he got the chance to. He'd pull his own shirt off, then lift the shirt of whomever he was fighting up over their head hockey-style so it pinched their arms to their torso, and he'd punch their faces until they bled, passed out, or both. It was a cocky, no-one-back-down mentality, and even among friends there was an eagerness to prove yourself to the pack that was maddening. Everybody was feigning alpha status. But Levi tried the hardest.

Jessie Roberts had the perfect family. His parents were still together, and his father had steady work as an accountant at Cutco. He had a big-breasted older sister named Rochelle, with long blond hair who drove a 1980 Subaru DL 4WD Wagon that he would get once she went to college. There was something very wholesome about his family life that we all wanted to be near, but we also hated him for it.

Jack VanderCamp was the oldest of us, about to turn eighteen. He was nicknamed "the Shark" because he once had an erection while doing the backstroke in front of everyone at a coed gym class. He had a scar on his abdomen from a bicycle wreck that embedded the uncovered metal end of the handlebar in his body. The scar looked like a white ringworm rash made of bubbled-up ham fat. Jack, even though he was blessed with a fluid athleticism on the field, always looked saddled, burdened like the world was about to fall on him. Girls loved him for this.

A few years earlier, Lewis and I had followed him and our older sister, Jamie, into the cemetery across the street from our house. From a distance, we watched him pull off her clothes, then take her breasts into his mouth. Even up until that point we were still going to tease Jamie about it later.

Then Jack bent Jamie backward over a headstone so her hair was swaying toward the ground and her feet were flailed out in front of her. He stuck his hand between her legs and started moving his fingers in and out of her like the pistons of a large machine.

I went silent, but Lewis started mumbling, calling her a slut in short breaths like he couldn't breathe and ran off toward our house. I wanted to run after him, to keep running, but he seemed so mad I was scared to go near him. I thought of running the other way, but my fingers dug under the grass like talons that kept me perched there snooping on my sister alone—a moment neither Lewis nor I would ever mention again.

In the winters when we were younger, we would throw snowballs at cars. One fall, a few of the guys dropped a pumpkin off a train bridge onto the windshield of a stranger's passing car. They could only describe the sounds of what happened next as they ran for their lives. On a long summer night, as eight of us were feeling very brave, we flipped a jade-green Studebaker. We let it fall on its side, then we pushed on the engine's covers so it fell onto its top, which slammed down, gave a few ticking sounds, and crunched in under its own weight.

Everyone called Shawn Nowak "Idiot Is Here." He had bragged about using an access ladder and climbing to the top of the town's enormous mushroom-shaped water tower and spray-painting swear words on top to insult low-flying airplanes. No one believed he had done it, and dismissed him entirely when he was caught telling different groups of kids that he'd immortalized different swear words up above. Though months later, when a city worker went up to check the tower they found *SHAWN NOWAK WAS HERE* scrawled in red paint from end to end of the tower. The police were called and they drove right to Shawn's house.

When word of what he'd done got out my group of friends immediately took to calling him "Idiot Is Here," whenever he walked into a room.

When I was alone with him once, I asked him what happened when the police arrested him.

"They never arrested me. I was too young."

"I heard you went to jail."

"No. The officer who came to my house kept telling my mom how dangerous what I'd done was. How I was up on this huge rounded globe without any rope. He was really worried about me. Kind of a nice guy, actually."

"Were you scared when you did it?"

"It was dark. I lay on my stomach and slid along from letter to letter. My sneakers sort of held tight to the sides. It wasn't until after that cop came and I went back to look up at how high up I really was that I got scared. I felt like an idiot. That's why I figured it was fine people called me that. A good reminder to never do something so stupid again."

I imagined the feeling of climbing rung by rung up through the dark, stomach-stuck to the downward curve, one deep, looping graffiti letter away from slipping off the edge with nowhere to land.

One day we found out Jack VanderCamp's father had been stabbed and killed at a bar in Tennessee. His mother had told Todd Hornick's mom about it, and Mrs. Hornick told everybody. None of us ever mentioned it. We were silent about our poverty and our tragedy, as talking would only cast light on the ragtag settlement we were, left in the debris of failed families.

Yet we continued to gather, straight-backed, slump-shouldered, and all smiles as if birthed from cold milk into easy lives—so eager to be friends that I had grown to love them for all they were to me, and all I could not find elsewhere. I had even become accustomed to our violent, cruel sort of football and loved the wild feeling it gave me. I kept that feeling locked inside me and tried to bash it out with the help of my friends. That was our ritual. But when Lenwood Murry showed up drunk off of cheap cordials he stole from his stepfather's bar, the Tavern, the rules of what we had been doing changed for good.

Len would frequently steal enough alcohol from his stepdad's bar that the rest of us could get blackout drunk. And though we might tackle each other when we were drunk, we never played drunk. Our football games were the only sacred thing we had, but Len started forcing himself into the games and after would start his bullying, pushing everyone around. I could hear it in everyone's voices that they wanted things put right.

The shag of Len's bangs brushed back off his gorilla forehead and revealed the fold of bone above his eyebrows. He had facial hair where the rest of us had soft fuzz, like on the happy trails hanging off our belly buttons, like bleached yarn. When Len went to tackle me I saw his dark eyes shadowed by that glaring forehead ridge. He picked me up, lifting my whole body on his shoulder, and drove me back into the ground. Then he palmed my chin and slammed the back of my head into the grass.

"You fuck," I murmured, trying to push his massive body off me. That's when he slammed his knee into my ribs so hard I knew that that yellow-blue meat color would set in and slowly waterfall off my rib cage.

He let me up, saying, "Watch your mouth."

"That was a cheap shot, you fat slob," I said.

Then he exploded. I hit a nerve, or more likely he had been waiting for the smallest provocation. He ran forward and drove his shoulder into the ribs he'd just kneed and planted me back into the dirt. I tried to elbow him in the temple, but the force of his body on mine knocked the wind out of me. I could see the cauliflower bumps of his back teeth and smell the adrenal sweat, staleness of old cigarettes, and sweet liquor on his breath as he sat on top of me and started pummeling his fists into my face. He landed enough solid punches that my right eye swelled shut.

He was swearing in a tirade over me as he ripped my shirt down from the hem of the neck so it hung off me like a shoulder cape. Then he grabbed my shorts by the waistline, gripping my underwear as well, and pulled them down around my ankles. He pulled my clothes off my legs as the group pulled him off me. I lay there on the ground in the rag of my shirt and my tattered old sneakers.

When I looked down to the small salted slug of my exposed penis, I tasted blood running down my throat. I stared at the circle my friends had formed around me for what felt like a long time. Then, realizing how badly I was hurt, I started crying, letting big bloody snot bubbles pop from my mouth and nose, and I bawled big inaudible whimpers as if I were a creature about to die. I cried for every sadness I ever held on to.

"Get lost, you puss," Len said.

I rolled onto my hands and knees and my whole world narrowed to the red *drip-drip-drip* falling from my lip.

"Too far," Shawn Nowak said.

"Fuck you, Idiot Is Here," Len said.

"What's wrong with you?" Levi Smith yelled.

"Fuck you, Levi."

There was a chorus of welling anger directed at Lenwood as I limped away. My nakedness could have easily been theirs, and they knew it. Len screamed again, "I'll take you all on!"

Something in my legs was shaking as I walked away from

them. Some fear or hurt or hatred that I couldn't hide. I held my right hamstring and quad to muffle a spasm. When I hunched over, my penis rested on my forearm and blood splattered on my feet.

When I looked back, Len stood in the middle of them all. They had circled him in solidarity of each other, in mutual protection. He stood flatfooted with his giant body swaying. He turned slowly. The swath of his stained T-shirt between his shoulder blades was wide as a billboard, and his hands were stretched out in front of him like a wrestler's. Everyone who was looking at his back would step closer, only to jump back when he swiveled toward them. In this way they danced around him like hungry but timid wolves. Then Len struck out, grabbed Jeff Malone by the shoulders, swung him around his hip like a Hula-Hoop, and launched him ten feet away. Jeff's head thudded into the dirt, and the circle shifted to enclose Len again.

"I'll take all of you," he yelled.

The circle pinched tighter. They were bloodthirsty, each wanting to tear something from Len.

By the time I was halfway to the trees everyone was pushing at Len; anyone who got close to him he sent flying. When he yelled, "I'm going to hold the next person who touches me solely responsible," I turned to watch.

What happened next is as clear in my mind now as any other benchmark of my life. My brother, Lewis, charged from somewhere outside the circle that formed around Len. He slammed his body against Lenwood's back and wrapped his arms around Len's throat and head. Lewis's face was fire-hydrant red as he locked his legs around Len's hips and squeezed his whole body into him.

Len spun with Lewis on his back. Lewis, who rarely said a word but would run and run and run until he passed out from heat stroke, had his eyes shut as Len's face went purple and he fell to his knees.

Jessie Roberts then ran forward and kicked Len in the head. When Jessie pulled back his leg, Len caught him, and bit into Jessie's shinbone. Jessie screamed while Lewis continued to choke the air out of Len, who was now gnawing on Jessie's leg.

The fight ended with Len out cold on his face. Lewis didn't open his eyes until he must have felt everything in Len spill into the grass. When Lewis stood up, there was something holy about his face. For a moment I thought Len was dead.

Then Lewis walked out of the circle and started in the direction of home, Jessie started to crawl away, and everyone else started peeling off the circle and heading off too. No one came looking for me where I was hiding in the trees.

Len lay on the ground.

The Buffalo Bills finished that year with a 52–21 loss to the Cincinnati Bengals and ended their season with a 2–14 record. I watched the last game by myself at my house. The sense that the Bills would disappoint me every year of my life set in, but I was too invested by then to shed them.

My desire to belong to the group of boys soon crested. Every time I looked in one of their eyes I had to swallow the shame of their seeing me so helpless. None of the boys told anyone else anything. But we all knew of the others' failures. Our mothers and sisters and girlfriends would blab and we'd hear. Not saying it ourselves was our only badge of courage, and to hold it all in and smash your way through was our bylaw. But that night with Len, I had failed. I had shown the ugly truth of the sad state we all were really in. In my nakedness and tears, I had unearthed the feeling that we were all being trapped by something we couldn't see, something that could take us at any moment—possibly our own brutality.

Jason McKillroy was killed in a car wreck before he even got out of high school. Fifteen of the twenty-seven of us joined the military. Each seeking money, or discipline, or some, I suspect, more violence. Most joined the army and a few joined the marines. Charlie Rutkowski, marines, was the first to be killed in action. His father spent the whole day of the funeral mowing his lawn. To all our surprise my brother, Lewis, signed up for the navy. I always figured he did that to get as far away from his family as he could. So when he ended up clear on the other side of the world, I was happy for him. It was only years later that I became angry with the military for poaching among the poor and taking my friends and family away.

I know at least three of those fifteen never made it out of their first tour in the service. Jeff Malone got a bullet lodged in his spine and lost the use of his legs after a friendly fire accident at Camp Lejeune. The rest have not had large or tragic enough events happen to them for news of their lives to reach me. I'm glad for that, as any one of their names brings it all flooding back, and I've tried to forget them all.

I went to Buffalo State like my sister, Jessie Roberts, and his sister, Rochelle. Jamie, who went through enrollment a few years earlier, helped me apply for financial aid. I did my best to start a new life. But I was always thinking of Lewis, especially during the bombing of Iraq, and what it was like for him being on decks of destroyers that were firing fourteen-inch guns toward the shore from six miles out at sea. I hoped that cracking salvo would be loud enough to bang out whatever screaming I knew he had deep in his heart.

When I think of those football games, I still see everyone circled around my naked body. I still feel the shame of my helplessness, like an inflamed and itchy scar running through my chest. And when the barometer drops, I feel the broken bones in my eye socket and find myself thinking of Lenwood Murry.

I waited there in the trees that night, like a wounded animal, until Len woke up. Everything was quiet; the cicadas had not yet started their soft songs. Grass had indented the side of his muted face. There were already a few stars. Part of me wanted to reach out and help him up, to leave a bloodied handprint on his shoulder. A mark of solidarity. I'm sure at that moment Len felt as if he, too, were all alone; must have known, as he hunched to his knees, that despite our games, despite the intimacy that comes from breaking bone and skin, we all truly are.

3

Connor Thurber, 1985

The cemetery across from our house on Sandalwood Avenue was another place Lewis and I frequently spent time shooting off fireworks and arrows, hunting among the gravestones for where they landed.

"Can't kill the dead twice," Lewis said, pulling an arrow from a skewered plot.

We played an insane sort of bicycle tag on the gravel path through the headstones that left us both road-rashed and be-jeweled with gravel. When it got dark we ran among the slabs and howled to hear our own voices hitting the open air. Once, Lewis was running ahead of me and hurdled the face of a thick marble headstone and disappeared behind it. When I caught up to him, I saw the pile of dirt he'd missed and found him on his hands and knees in the open grave.

When he stood up, his head was the only thing not under-ground, and there was a splotch of mud on his forehead.

"Is it scary?" I asked.

"For shit-sure," Lewis said. "Help me out of here."

I grabbed the waistline of his shorts when he jumped up and folded his stomach over the lip of the plot. His foot made a sucking sound where it got caught in the mud. "I lost my shoe," Lewis said. When he was out we both stood over the hole and looked into it. "Should we say a prayer?" He jabbed my arm and started running again, his muddy sock loose at the toes and slapping the ground with each step.

Our father had given Lewis the high-tension bow-and-arrow before he left. It was something Lewis and I never spoke of, but I remembered every second of that day and played it over and over, looking for clues I'd missed. Our father had already said goodbye to me and Jamie and was in the driveway of our house talking to Lewis, who looked like a quickly deflating balloon. His shoulders were sagging with everything Dad said. The bow was in his left hand, and the tip was scratching the blacktop. From the porch where I had ducked behind the bushes, I couldn't hear what they were saying. Then our father got into his powder-blue Oldsmobile, open duffel bags full of his clothes overflowing from the back seat, which was also stuffed with tools, files, a bison skull, a stack of hardcover novels without their dust jackets, and heaps of philosophy books he'd stolen from the Olean Public Library.

After years of fighting, dealing with our mother's sloppy drinking, and his own failed attempts to stay sober, our father pulled away and went west. He told us he'd accepted a job running power lines for Alberta-Montana Power Company near Kalispell. He closed his firework store on the interstate and moved the contents that hadn't sold into a storage unit. And that was it. He left.

Lewis had this crazy-pale face as he walked back toward the house.

"What's going on?" I asked.

"Dad got a better-paying job," he told me. His voice didn't break when he said it, but he didn't look at me. Then his body twisted around like he was trying to find a way for those words to settle so he could believe them.

"Why now?" I asked.

"Don't worry about it."

"What do you mean 'don't worry about it'? How can I not worry about it?" I said, but I knew from Lewis's glare that I was once again earning my new nickname.

"You're a waste of skin," he'd told me a few months earlier. From that, he worked out his random furies on me with "Skinboy," which had taken the place of my name.

"Leave me alone, Skinboy," Lewis said as he turned and pushed me away from him. I tripped over a discarded birdhouse and fell back on the grass in our cluttered backyard. Jamie was watching us from the backroom, where she'd set up an architect's desk for painting. Jamie had a new group of friends she'd been spending more and more time with. But whenever she was home, she was in that room painting. She was good, too. She had been working on a painting of a woman's body in white clothes floating above the gravestones in a cemetery. The woman seemed to be lifted up by her breastbone so her hair fell back to the earth. The only thing not painted yet was the woman's face, which I expected to be happy or transcendent. I could tell Jamie was listening to us through the open window. And though she usually yelled at Lewis for hurting me, she said nothing. From the grass I watched as he disappeared into the house, which was a maroon color with curls of dried paint that fell in chips like dandruff.

"I want to go where Dad's going," I said to Jamie.

"Me too," she said through the window.

The only time we consistently saw our mother was one night a month when people in our town put their large trash items on the curb for the sanitation department to pick up the next morning. Our neighbors would drag out old Whirlpool appliances, ironing boards, and whatever else the weekly garbage truck couldn't take. On those evenings, our mom loaded us into her rusted-over, white 1970 Chevy Caprice station wagon, with its vinyl side panel, and we'd slowly cruise the streets picking through the refuse.

I'd get this fishbowl feeling as she slowed down and parked in front of those houses. Each home gave off a sense of neatness and order that seeped into their lawns. I always felt like they were looking out their windows at us, which made me want to pull my lower lip over my head and swallow myself whole. That's probably why Jamie never came with us. But my mom and Lewis were unfazed by what other people thought as she gingerly picked discarded rabbit-ear antennas, steel rods, sheet metal, chicken wire, aluminum siding, large bolts, coffee cans, aluminum fruit jars, and every scrap of metal or iron and tossed them in the back of the Caprice.

She'd walk from lawn to lawn on the sidewalk while Lewis and I took turns inching the car along beside her. I was so young when we started doing this that on my turns I'd nudge the gas pedal and brake with my tiptoes. I wasn't big enough to see over the steering column, so I navigated through the line of sight between the dashboard and the top of the enormous steering wheel. When we had to cross an intersection, she'd get back in, drive across, and we'd start down the next block.

I was always getting stabbed by the jagged metal edges of the things we collected on our rounds. If she needed help lifting anything, my mom took a pair of my dad's worn work gloves and tossed them onto my lap. I'd wiggle my fingers in the extra space of each finger sleeve, and that extra room would knot up or twist against what we were lifting so it looked like I had a man's hands that had been pummeled by a hammer. We'd toss what we found in the back, where it would shake the suspension and clank against everything else. Once, after doing this, my mother ran her hand up the back of my neck so her palm feathered up my hairline. It shocked me that her hands were not rough or calloused. Even with her bandanna and frayed clothes, she was a woman whom men always found attractive. She had an accent, which men found exotic. They would ask me or Lewis, when she wasn't looking, "Where's she from?"

Tiny, the neighborhood vet who lit the bonfire at homecoming, had asked once, and ever since he'd call out, "Hello, German Lady," whenever he saw us. Tiny was a pack rat. I heard Lewis say there was medicine that could help cure him, but people in town always talked about Tiny like he was a news story, and I'm not sure what about him was really true or what Lewis was just repeating. I know that he probably had a glandular problem that made him so large, that his Grizzly Adams beard covered half the *A* on the 1960s letterman sweater he wore everywhere, that the line of gunk around the bifocal cut of his apple-size glasses was solid and yellowish-brown. The police were in the habit of arresting him for one day each fall. They'd claim he broke some sort of county ordinance. And then the city would bring out a backhoe and garbage truck to clean up his yard. His blue Suburban with both bumpers and three doors held together by rope and duct tape was filled to the roof with trash that burst out the windows.

Sometimes, Tiny's blue Suburban and my mother's station wagon would end up on the same street, trawling opposite sides of the road until they'd meet toward the middle. Then I could see how Tiny's whole face scrunched up each time he manically blinked, and how that lifted and dropped his beard like a curtain over the middle button of his sweater. "Hello, German Lady," he said.

We tried not to talk to Tiny. There was something mangled-up in his voice, and even though I didn't recognize it at the time as being lustful toward my mother, it made me not like him. If Tiny was close, I'd get out of the car and help my mother and Lewis. I took the odd protective energy I was feeling and focused it on trying to claim all the best trash before he did, as if we were in some twisted arms race. I'd place extra value on useless things for the sake of competition and insist that we add what I'd found to our pile. Then, all of a sudden, it dawned on me that I was in a stranger's yard. I'd look up and see neighbors tucked behind their curtains looking at us. I'd look around and see my mother,

Lewis, and Tiny, and wonder if we were all in need of some med-
ication to make us better.

Once, in the middle of that summer, my mother, Lewis, and I
were driving around town, and she was trying to get Lewis to
start calling me Connor again.

"Skinboy is not a nice name for such a sweet boy. I don't like
it," she said. She looked at me through the rearview mirror. "You
know, when you were really little I'd hear you through the door
singing these nursery rhymes. I'd peek my head in to tell you to
sleep, and you'd be humming and singing with your eyes shut.
You'd be breathing heavy but still singing. I hear that still, you
know, hear you singing. It's a good sound to have in my head,"
she said. "Maybe if I sneak in with Lewis and we hear you sing in
your sleep, then he won't call you such an ugly nickname."

I knew she would never find out because, even if she was at
home, she was always so loud at night, clopping around with big
heavy steps, falling into walls, and crying or singing her own self
to sleep.

That night, we found a pile of twelve-foot steel rebar poles
on someone's lawn. We each took an end of one and tried to
slide them into the back of the Caprice. The poles wobbled in
the middle, so Lewis stood between us and supported them. We
struggled to get three into the back. None of us saw Tiny park in
front of the next house. I jumped when I realized he was on the
other side of the pile. He bent down next to the pile of rebar and
wrapped his arms around it, letting his fingers dig into the ground
and burrow underneath the poles, and lifted the whole pile.

"Hey, we found those first," Lewis said. My mother put

her hand on his shoulder, which he shrugged off, but she'd quieted him.

The rebar must have weighed well over a hundred pounds, but Tiny's face didn't strain at all. He spun so the tip of the pile facing in front of him was aimed at the back of our car. He walked forward so the pile slid right on top of the three poles we'd put in already. As he shimmied the poles farther into the back of our car, the wheel well dipped closer to the street.

"Wow," my mother said, "thank you."

Tiny brushed the rusted metal dust off his sleeves and stuck out his hand toward my mother. His forearm was the size of my waist.

My mother lifted her hand to shake his.

But instead of stopping, he reached his hand toward her chest with all his fingers together and facing up. Then he flicked his hand underneath my mother's left breast.

"What the—" my mother spit out as she jumped back and slapped his hand away.

Lewis shot toward Tiny, and I saw his foot heave back behind his body, winding up to kick. My mother reached out and blocked Lewis's chest so his kick missed Tiny's kneecap. I watched without knowing what to do as Tiny turned back to his Suburban.

"*You can't do that!*" Mom yelled.

"I hate you," Lewis screamed, and I could hear the start of tears and something horrible in his voice before he choked it back. My mother stood behind him and draped her arms over his shoulders—scarfing him in a hug.

I waited in the car as my mother led Lewis to the back seat. She put her hands on his cheeks and whispered something to him I couldn't hear. As she walked around to the driver's seat, Lewis looked at me and whispered, "You're a pussy, Skinboy."

I sat quietly as we drove away, our mother turning the car on a wide sloping angle so the seven feet of rebar protruding from the back wouldn't scrape against anything.

At the end of those gathering excursions, we drove all the way to the old warehouse in downtown Buffalo that had been converted into lofts. We helped her drag everything into her studio and added to the piles of metal from our previous trips that lined the scuffed drywall. She'd splattered the walls in bright purple and pale orange paints. There was an old couch and mattress in the corner and workbenches covered in canvases, squeezed tubes of oil paints, and plastic liquor bottles everywhere else. We never stayed long. If we met other people in the hall she ushered us out quickly after introducing us as her sons.

"She's probably ashamed of you two creeps," Jamie told me.

The studio was a place our mother went to disappear. There, she lived a life other than the one she lived with us. There, she would take the materials gathered and arc weld gigantic abstract sculptures. When she came back to us with new work, I pictured her bending into the shower of molten orange sparks bouncing off the dark faceplate of her helmet—the blue-tongued coalescence of metals drawing her closer to something that only she'd seen among the junk piles. I'd study the beaded melding points of her work, how each joint somehow balanced heavy materials in intricate and subtle curves that she'd spray-paint vivid colors so the whole thing looked like electrified raw minerals geysering from the earth.

She displayed her work, in craft fairs or galleries, but most of her sculptures never sold and ended up hidden by a seven-foot wooden fence in our backyard. One of those sculptures had three twelve-foot strips of curved iron balancing against each other on a pivot that kept them moving like waves. One day, I bent one of the tips of the metal wave down so it bowed into the grass and launched gravel twenty feet in the air when it sprung back.

I wanted to knock down our fence so people could see we had a sculpture garden and not a junkyard. Or better yet, I wanted to be able to pick the fence up over my head and place it around my family at various moments of my choosing, showing only what I wanted to, controlling how we were perceived.

I'd lift the fence up and show my mother wielding the blue flame. Then I'd slam the fence down around her gathering trash. I wanted to take my fence and lock it around Tiny so no one in my family would ever see that son of a bitch again. I'd slam it around my mother in our front yard that summer after someone spray-painted *TRASH WHORE* on the sidewalk just before the Fourth of July parade. She tried to clean it by pouring gasoline on the concrete slabs to burn it off, but the match lit a flame that shot ten feet over her head.

"What's she doing?" I heard Jamie gasp from where she stood next to Lewis at the living room window. Our mother had come inside crying and told us about the graffiti. She went outside cursing something in German that I didn't understand, and seconds later the street shot up in flames.

From inside the house, we could hear people driving past, honking and calling our mom a nut as she dolloped more gas onto the corner like a magician whose trick had gone horribly wrong. As I watched her, I had the image of insatiable orange flames spreading across the leaves on the ground—each leaf igniting at the stem, burning bright orange and touching the next leaf, and the next, until I could hear someone's voice saying, "Your mother burned down the neighborhood."

The next night, after sorting through what she did and did not want from our most recent scavenger trip, our mother loaded me and Lewis into the Caprice and drove us to the back of the cemetery, where the north and west borders met and dropped off a sloping ravine into the Allegheny River. She backed up to the cliff, next to the tree with the No Dumping sign screwed into it, opened the back hatch of the car, and had us help her toss the contents off the hill. I heaved the ceramic tops of toilet bowls, moldering boxes of old *National Geographic* magazines, and a box of rusted lighting fixtures.

Lewis pointed to the sign on the tree so our mother would see.

"You're too young, and I'm too foreign to get in trouble," she told us. "We're the perfect team," she assured us as glossy photos of African elephants, South American jungles, and outer space fluttered down the gorge.

At the bottom of the ravine, there was a small path that ran along the river. Lewis and I had walked it many times. It was another place where we went to shoot off fireworks. Lewis taught me how to lick my finger and pass it back and forth through the

Zippo's flame. It was there we'd watched whistlers shoot off orange into the night and we swore the sparks floated downstream on the water.

It was that trail Lewis would bring me to three nights later. He led the way without telling me why we were walking. The water was brown but still clear enough to see the waving algae coating the rocks, rounded and resting on each other under the surface. Kingbirds and finches flew from tree to tree in the canopy over our heads. Some of the trees shot out of the ravine at odd angles, searching for light.

"I found something," Lewis kept telling me when I asked where we were going.

He led me between the side of the ravine and the winding river. I knew we'd passed the strip mall parking lot from the industrial dumpsters on the upper edge of the hillside. We went another few miles until I wasn't sure what street we would have found if we climbed the hill.

It was getting dark when Lewis said, "Let's climb up here." He pointed to a small water runoff cut into the slope of the ravine. He started up first. His feet kicked scree and clumps of dirt onto me. After fifty feet of climbing we had to use the tree branches to pull ourselves up the rest of the way, from branch to branch until the grade wasn't so steep and it curved slowly into a wooded area. "Crouch down." Lewis was now running ahead of me with his body bent over his legs like he was falling. I did the same thing as best I could but fell twice. I followed him along the lip of the ravine until he dived into a pile of leaves ahead of him. "Down," he said, and I dived in after him.

We army-crawled another twenty feet until we came to the back of a house closer to the road. The porch light shone on the yard. The porch was covered in cords of wood and black and white garbage bags heaped on top of each other. There were wooden pallets strewn across the yard loaded with mounds of old plastic toys, reams of used and moldering papers, TV antennas, and ironing boards.

Then I saw the blue Suburban.

Lewis grabbed my wrist so I couldn't slip back down the hill. I hunkered lower into the dirt slope behind the house. "I saw his car when I was biking home the other day and followed him here. I saw the river ran behind his house and I knew we could find it from the trail."

"Okay, now can we get out of here?"

"Wait. I've got to show you something."

We army-crawled the crescent moon-shaped swath of Tiny's backyard.

"Here. Come here," Lewis called. Fifty yards from the house, his yard started sloping into the ravine, and we rested our stomachs on the lip of the decline. There was a clearing in the junk piles and a straightaway to Tiny's back porch.

It took me a moment to realize that what he wanted to show me was right next to him and not in the yard. There was a large brown tarp spread out over the ground. Lewis kneeled next to it and yanked it back, letting it fall loose behind him. There must have been two hundred empty soda and beer cans and liquor bottles. They were tucked close to each other at an angle facing Tiny's house. Each bottle was loaded with various sizes of larger fireworks. The whole thing looked like an organ in some hobo church.

"Jesus!"

Lewis took a key from his pocket and let it dangle in front of me. "It's the key to dad's fireworks storage unit I stole. I've been setting up for the last three nights." He crawled below the firework organ and rooted around behind a bush. When he came back, he had his bow and four arrows in his right hand, and in his left was one of Mom's handheld blowtorches. I'd seen her cut through strips of steel with it.

"We're going to get him!" Lewis said.

"What does that mean?" I asked. Lewis started adjusting the trajectory of the fireworks the tarp had misaligned. "This isn't funny."

"You going to be a waste of skin your whole life?" Lewis spat at me. There was a wild and quick anger in his voice when he spoke. "We have to do this," he said.

"Why?"

"Our mother let other men touch her," Lewis said, pointing the charred chrome end of the torch at me.

"She didn't *let* Tiny touch her," I said.

"No, Dad told me," he said.

"Dad wasn't there."

"No. He told me that before he moved. He said, 'Your mother let other men touch her.'" The words oozed out like a yeasty blood clot that had been sealed away until now. Lewis's eyes were welling up, and he was gnashing his teeth so the tendons in his neck were popping.

"What would Dad do if he saw what Tiny did?" he asked.

I'm not sure what else we whispered to each other in the dark, his sternness pushing through my fear, until he convinced me to stand twenty yards away from him with the bow and arrow. On his mark, I set the forked tail of the arrow against the bow's string and drew it back. Lewis wanted me to shoot it at Tiny's back door. In both our minds it was a clean shot that resounded through the house and left the arrow shaking at the end. But when I let it go, the string slapped a slice of my forearm skin away and the arrow wobbled ten yards ahead of me and landed sideways.

"Try again," Lewis whisper-yelled as I dropped to my knees and realized how bad the cut on my inner forearm hurt.

After I missed with two more arrows, I watched as Lewis threw a rock against Tiny's porch. Then he threw another, and a third. On the fifth stone, the back door opened and Tiny walked out. He was shirtless and wasn't wearing glasses. I fell forward on my chest trying as hard as I could to blend into the ground.

The first firework shot red and orange out of the woods and went over Tiny's house. Lewis was running the blue-lit end of the blowtorch over the tops of all the bottles. The wicks were simmering orange before they ignited, and firework after firework started bombarding Tiny's house. The forest sounded like an angry god. *Pop-pop-pop.* Echoes rebounding. *Pop-pop-pop.* Sizzling streaks of fire cut the gray smoke. Each breath pulled in the scent of burned powder, which scratched the back of my throat. Missiles of color exploded and slowly fell over one another. White, yellow, and red, and each large explosion was broken by a dozen whistlers and Roman candles raining onto Tiny. Smoke and bursts of orange sparks clouded my vision, but I could still see Lewis's white eyes, flared nostrils, and corded neck. His feet were planted wide apart, and he appeared to tremble either from nerves or the strange lights splintering the dark.

Tiny stood unflinching on the porch as an arsenal was going off all around him. Lewis was dancing around the firework organ, wholly caught up in the wondrousness of his fiery creation. I could see him moving through the trails of smoke rising in the darkened woods.

Tiny didn't look scared as much as frozen. A giant firework could have hit him in the head and he wouldn't have moved. Lewis's aim sent explosions on and right before the porch, and whistlers were bounding off the house and ricocheting off the roof. *We might kill him or burn down his house,* I thought. Lewis danced as if that was exactly what he had come to do.

My brother made a guttural roaring *ahaa* sound as the last of the fireworks were shooting off, and I saw Tiny's head snap toward Lewis, as if he'd just woken up. Tiny took one step forward and then was off the porch and running. The echo of the fireworks were drowned out by my thrashing heartbeat hammering in my ears. I yelled for Lewis, or, I tried to yell. I hoped I'd given some beat of warning as I grabbed the bow and the last arrow and sprinted directionless back into the dark woods to save myself.

Tiny chased us down the gorge to the river. I heard him crashing downhill behind us—heavy breaths and sticks breaking. My clothes kept catching and tearing on branches and a bramble bush scratched the right side of my face. Lewis passed me as we ran down the ravine and was moving so quickly he couldn't stop and he launched himself into the river—splashing and running across the rounded-smooth rocks, struggling toward the other side. I turned in time to run along the trail on the bank. Behind me, I heard an even louder splash. I jumped off the trail and started climbing up the ravine wall, lost a shoe, and kept pulling myself up between the trees—moving branch by branch, some breaking and splintering pieces of bark taking scraps of skin from my hand. I tucked in beside a tree and looked down.

Tiny was in the water. He lumbered forward, and his right leg rolled on a rock and he slipped. The river consumed his gigantic body. When he came back up he made a wild gasping sound. Lewis's shadow was climbing up the other side of the hill in the trees and brush. My heart was pounding, and I hid farther behind the tree and watched as Tiny slowly spun around in the water. I could make out every detail of his body in the moonlight, the matted-down hair up his arms and across his pillar-size chest, tucking under that epic, now dripping beard.

"I hate you!" I heard Lewis scream from the opposite hillside.

Tiny turned toward Lewis's side of the ravine. I was too petrified to move in case he would see me.

"I hate you!" Lewis's voice rang out again.

Lewis sounded crazy with meanness. Tiny started walking upstream, his legs lumbering against the soft current. He stumbled forward but set his feet to hold himself upright. I had no idea what he would do if he caught one of us and the mystery of what was in his head made my stomach gurgle up into my throat. I could taste the words our father had said to Lewis, and suddenly understood why he looked so blank and broken as our father pulled out of our driveway to leave. *Your mother let other men touch her.* My shoulder blades dug farther into the tree, and for a moment, I was overwhelmed by the very real sense that I might be terrified for the rest of my life.

I turned so the tree was still hiding most of my body. My chest leaned into the knotted folds of bark, and I kept an arm ringed around it as I stepped out of its shadow.

I laced in my last arrow, held the bow in front of me, and pulled the string back.

"I hate you!" I squeezed out of my locked chest as the taut string snapped loose from my hand.

The arrow wobbled loose ahead of me but hit a sapling and was lost in the brush before it made it to the river.

Tiny turned up toward me, and through the dark I saw his wet hair against his forehead. He was outlandish and hulking as he scanned the hillside.

Lewis screamed again.

Tiny turned toward him.

I screamed.

Lewis and I echoed each other as Tiny stood in the water and listened to the banks yelling at him.

In the water, Tiny looked mystified by the strangeness of what was happening. Part of me felt bad for him.

I stopped screaming. Lewis did not.

Lewis screamed in short staccato-popping rhythms the same phrase over and over again. He was showing me how to purge everything that was bottled up, and having also screamed I knew how it felt, but Lewis was still full of so much more than I could comprehend.

It was Lewis who scared me most when I turned back up the hillside, digging into the dirt with my fingers and the tip of the bow. The dirt was cool and the pine needles on the ground pricked the outer layers of my skin. Every few steps I slipped as the dirt ravine wall got steeper and I reached for a root or branch to pull myself up.

There was no moon as I breached the gulch, just a tree-lined street that I had never been on and did not know where it led. I took a right and ran over the smooth blacktop. I ran as far as I could and then started walking when I realized the street no longer followed the river. I kept walking toward the direction I thought our house was, looking for anything that was familiar. But all the houses seemed different to me in the dark than any of the ones I stopped in front of and collected trash with my mother. I tried to look into all the darkened windows as I walked the streets until morning, feeling the tears in my clothes and scrapes in my skin as if I was molting something— shedding who I had been.

4

Catrin Thurber, 1986

Years ago, before things got really bad, Terrance skipped work on a Wednesday and we took the kids to Wendt Beach on Lake Erie. We must not have paid attention to the weather, as it was one of those cool, gray days, with a low sky, that randomly break up the warm summer months. The wind at the far end of the beach was picking up plumes of sand that looked like giant tan feathers. The feathers dissolved in the distance and came blowing down the empty strand, scrubbing our faces, so we had to squint and walk with our heads down. The waves were only slowly lapping at the shore early that morning, but it looked like they had been pounding in overnight and had washed a large swath of drift-wood all the way up the beach against the high grass dunes.

Jamie wanted to go home immediately, but the boys were al-ready chasing each other along the shore. Terrance and I spread out one blanket and wrapped a larger one over our heads and shoulders with Jamie tucked in between us.

Lewis and Connor were running back toward us and falling into the wind. Their shaggy hair was pulled back off their heads and shimmying wildly. Lewis tripped and dug his hands into the sand to crawl forward. They were laughing, and Jamie started laughing too when Terrance told her, "You've got a great seat to watch your brothers blow away."

When the boys reached us, they crawled under our blanket. Connor was sitting on my lap. Lewis was draped across Jamie and Terrance, and his feet were touching mine. We tucked the blanket in under each of us so that it draped over our heads like a tent.

"I don't think this wind is ever going to stop," Jamie said.

"I can do a rain dance if you want something else to happen," Lewis said.

The wind sounded hollow, and we all stopped talking as if we'd mutually decided to sit and listen. We were the only people on the beach, but the wind searched for us, and it wrapped that blanket tight around our bodies as if we were the only people in the world.

Later in the morning, when the wind died down, I had Terrance go back to our station wagon and get some of our tools. He brought three hammers, a box of six-inch nails, and a screw gun with screws. We each made a pile by pulling gnarled logs and branches off the sand drifts toward the middle of the beach. Each arthritic piece was smooth, water-varnished, and a soft brown with a deep reddish brown at the knots. We worked on one pile at a time, nailing and screwing the driftwood logs together, making tripods and four-corner bases by lining up whatever joints we could. From there we built up and outward with the thinner branches until it got top-heavy, tipped, and resettled. Then we kept adding more knotted wood, binding the random scraps until the logs bloomed up like an ancient tree.

We worked our way from pile to pile down the beach making the sculptures. Terrance was showing Connor how to carve shapes into the wood with the hammer's claw. Jamie and Lewis pushed one of the wood sculptures over. It caught in the sand and stood there in a different shape. Then they pushed it over again and again until it was in the lake. It was buoyant and bobbed on the surface.

When it got warmer that afternoon the boys went in the water. They leaned against the floating wood and started kicking their legs to push it farther out.

"Boys, that's far enough," I yelled to them. Connor dropped off the log and swam back with those wild overhead strokes that always exhausted him. Lewis kept kicking the wood tangle in a slow arc back to shore.

Connor got out, his suit matted to his skinny legs. "I'll dry myself off," he said, and spun himself around in quick circles, his arms flailed out. "I twirl—I twirl," he yelled.

When Lewis swam ashore, Terrance walked toward the boys with a towel but they started running away. Their father chased them among our sculptures, which looked like giant freaky spiders climbing out of the surf. They weaved between them and called to me and Jamie to help, which we did, and all of us chased one another through the obstacles we'd made. We yelled one another's names until our voices settled on the blowing sand and were carried away on the wind.

5

Lewis Thurber, 1986

My mom stood in the middle of the Greyhound station. She kept checking that the departure time hadn't changed. My ticket was all the way to Kalispell, Montana, where I would call my father from a pay phone and he'd come get me. He'd been writing and asking me to come visit him for years. And now there had been some trouble between me and my mother. Me and the people at school. Everyone wanting to shape my life. In my bag I had a stack of college applications my guidance counselor forced on me because to everyone's astonishment I'd aced the verbal SAT section. Prior to that no one thought much of my grades or potential. They didn't know about the storage unit of old books I grew up reading. But in my bag I also had enlistment papers for all four branches of the military. I knew my mother wouldn't sign any one of them and I thought perhaps I could get my long-lost father to do so.

My mom was so nervous seeing me off she couldn't stop blabbering. She talked so much I didn't really think to tell her how I was feeling. Maybe that's an excuse though. I knew I hadn't been easy on her. That I'd been giving her a tough time lately. I didn't tell her I was terrified of going to Montana. Of seeing my father.

We waited in the black bucket chairs with the pay-by-the-quarter TVs attached.

"When you went to kindergarten you took the bus to school," she said. She reached over and held my hand. "The bus driver at the time was a grandfather type named George, who was famous for yanking loose baby teeth from the kids he picked up. Apparently, everyone knew he did this, and any kid with a suspect tooth would open their mouths and present it to him as they stepped onto his bus.

"'What about this one,' they'd choke out with their mouths opened wide. 'Hummm, we'll let that one set for a while more,' George would say, unless the tooth was ready. Then, he'd reach his fat fingers into those kids' mouths, feeling for the exposed socket beneath the roots, and yank them out.

"'A nice one you got here,' he told them, and held it up for the child to inspect.

"When I first heard about George I imagined some total creep with a pile of baby teeth in his apartment and thought someone should call the police on him. I asked a woman who stood with me in the morning with her kids about him.

"'Oh, George is a harmless old sweetheart. He even has a paper towel roll next to his seat so these kids can sop up their blood, which I guess is kind of gross,' that lady said.

"George's bus wheezed to a stop at our corner, and I watched you march up the stairs, and like that, you were gone for the day, already living your own life, in a world where the bus driver pulls teeth, and there are any number of unaccountable oddities in wait for you. God, I was so scared for you then."

I looked over and saw her face was blotchy and red. She must have felt a warmth flushing up her neck as her fingers kept tapping at her throat. Her eyes kept blinking the way she did when she was trying not to cry.

"I feel the same way now," she said.

She had my hand, and I know she was being honest, which pierced me somehow, and I felt everything that was messy or hurt between us well up in me. I'd been so scared about seeing my father that I let my guard down around my mother, who I saw all the time. I turned away from her because I felt exposed and raw in the face of how much love she still had for me.

"Every day you got on that bus I'd say some version of a prayer, or at least a small meditation, where I asked the oddities to be kind to my kid until I could see you again. I feel like asking that now."

I had to go wash my face in the bathroom after she told me this, and when I took a minute to think of how she must be feeling, with me starting to really go away from her in life, it felt like she had set some deep hook in me, and I didn't like it. I was already full of such corroded hooks.

When I walked back to where she was sitting, she was rifling through my bag.

"Mom."

"Making sure you packed everything you need. Underwear and all that."

"I did."

"Well. I'm your mother. I'm going to mother you right till you get on the bus."

And she did. She was glued to my side and kept holding my hand and squeezing my shoulder.

When I finally hugged her and marched up the wheel well onto the bus, I sat by the window facing her. She stood without moving behind the big bus station window. Watching her, I remembered how we went to Kmart when I was little and she bought me a twenty-eight-inch aluminum Easton baseball bat. Then we went to the baseball diamond at the park. She pitched our one ball to me, and if I hit it she'd run after it and back to the mound. If I missed she'd run back to the backstop and get the ball. Our game mostly entailed her running, and she seemed to enjoy it as much as I did. I waved as the bus pulled away. I could see she was still trying not to cry and felt all her heavy energy radiating out to me.

As soon as the bus turned out of sight I felt better. Somehow lighter. I watched the lights out the window for the first leg of the trip. I'm not even sure I was thinking of anything all the way through Erie and onto Cleveland, where the interstate did this crazy ninety-degree left turn right in the middle of the city. The bus climbed an elevated byway, and I looked down at the stadiums and city buildings and felt the full magnitude of the trip I was on and who I was going to see come crashing down on me again.

When my father left us, he returned west to the mountains of Montana where he grew up. I didn't know it at the time, but my mother was damn near drinking herself to death. My father had been trying to keep up with her, but slammed on the brakes and peeled off from our family in what he claimed was a panicked attempt to save himself. Since then, the West has always been looming in the distance as a place you could disappear, or reinvent yourself, or whatever it was he had done. He had been sending me weekly letters since he left, and though I never wrote him back, I allowed them to construct some sort of life for him, that I always longed for myself.

I tried to think like I was going to glimpse some new place for my life on that sixty-three-hour bus ride. But on the bus, a dreadful tiredness set in as we passed through Davenport and Des Moines, Iowa; Omaha and Grand Island, Nebraska. I kept thinking of the man who left us. Of the shed full of fireworks and books he left behind. How I'd burned through both and felt no closer to him. I kept feeling more and more anxious. I went to dig out my list of applications from my bag to have something to read and saw they'd been rearranged. My file of military enlistment forms was missing. All that was left was the navy form, which I had taken out and put with the college applications I intended to throw away. I remembered my mother going through my bag back at the station and I felt a sudden fury with her for trying to steer my life, like she'd done such a good job with her own. It made me want to escape from my family and never make a decision to please another person again as long as I lived.

So, in Cheyenne, Wyoming, still furious, I got off the bus, and instead of getting on the transfer, I walked through the snow and dark and checked into a Motel 6 off the highway. I can't explain exactly why I did this, but I remember feeling like I was far enough away from my mother and not yet close enough to my father that I could really think about what I wanted to do for myself without their influence. I was feeling brave as I tossed my bag next to the bed, but that passed as soon as I sat down and realized my bus had probably already left.

I spent that night and all the next day in my room watching TV. Sort of scared of the world outside the door. Sort of feeling a bit crazy for what I'd done. I called my mom and told her but felt immediately ashamed of seeing myself as some sort of coward. Maybe for not going on with the trip. Or not wanting to go back. Not wanting to face anyone.

"Oh, Lewis," she said. "Just come home then. Get the next bus and come on home."

But the next morning, instead of getting on the bus I walked around the town. When I got back to the motel and paid for another night, there was a message from my mom.

"Your father will come get you. Tell him exactly where you are. He'll drive out."

I called her back and told her no. I didn't want that. I'd get a bus home. But I didn't plan on doing that either. I stayed in the motel and the next morning wandered the town and ended up in the local library to get out of the cold. I stayed inside and started looking at the newspaper rack and in the locals section I started reading the job ads.

That's where I found the ad for doing ranch work off Dead Hawk Highway.

Joe, the ranch manager, had posted a vague description of the work in the newspaper and I was the first person to call. He drove down to meet me. After we talked, he made a few background-check phone calls using my social security number and then hired me on the spot. Part of me wondered if he felt sorry for me, or knew I was in need of some sort of help. Whatever his motive, he drove me to a Girl Scouts ranch. The job offered a cabin to live in, which gave me someplace to spend my time until I figured out what to do with myself, or turned eighteen and could sign away my own fate.

When I first arrived and started working at the ranch, I spent my time off staring out my cabin windows, absorbing the white loneliness of that mountain field. It was too cold to go anywhere even if I had a car, and that trapped feeling got me so cooped up, I longed to wander off on the snow-covered mountainside and disappear. After I'd called my mother to tell her what I was doing, but not where I was, she told me she'd take care of my diploma. The only thing in the cabin to occupy me was a bunch of old books about how to be an outdoorsman that categorized all the trees and animals.

There was a book called *Pertaining to Sparrows* written by a woman who must have loved those birds more than anything else in the world. She wrote about the sparrows' predators as if she were afraid of such birds herself. She described a small falcon called a kestrel, with its rusty blue-gray cap and lightly spotted breasts, and the way it beat its wings before swooping down on smaller birds or insects, making a shrill *killy-killy-killy* noise. There were other books that spoke of the migration cycles and showed pictures of Steller's jays, purple martins, rock wrens, goldfinches, and grackles. I sat looking out that frozen window trying to imagine all those birds returning, calling to each other through the canopy of the subalpine forest. *Shee-e-e-e, C-Ough—C-Ough, killy-killy-killy*.

During the days, the only way I could settle down was to keep my hands busy, and keep my mind focused on plowing the road, or cleaning the facilities center. Then we started rewiring the electricity in the camper cabins, installing a new furnace for the activities center, building new partitions for the horse barn, and by May, I had passed the dregs of winter immersing myself in any project Joe had for us. If I was lucky, I would have worked hard enough during the day to be exhausted enough to sit contently on the deck at night. I could ease back into the rocking chair and let the night settle around me—listen to the new language of daily work, silence, and the wind carrying the sounds of life off the mountain.

In the summer, the older Girl Scouts kicked out the screens of their bunkhouse at night and wandered the open fields at the back part of the ranch. They often walked down the dirt road my cabin was on to get to the horse pasture. I could see them in the dark. They moved like timid deer—taking quick dashes ten yards at a time and stopping to assess the night around them. They betrayed themselves by laughing when one bumped into the other. I kept my porch light off so I could see the stars. The girls never paid attention to my cabin tucked along the tree line or me sitting on the deck as they lined up along the fence of the pasture, stepping on the first plank to lean over the top and coo to the horses. They waved carrots and apples they hoarded from the mess hall. I liked watching them—the slow saunter of the horses approaching and nuzzling the girls; their movements breaking the stillness of the night, fireflies touching the space around them like thin blue flames.

By morning, the girls made their way back to their bunks, and the horses were slick with dew and honey-colored in the pasture. The bear grass bloomed like fists of light pounding up the hillside, and by afternoon, rainstorms darkened the sky and struck the ground with lightning before blowing over and leaving a calm I have only felt in the mountains.

My boss, Joe, rented the horses from an outfit called Sombrero that let them free-range in the mountains during the fall and winter. The horses were all starved and half-wild by spring, when they came to the Girl Scouts ranch. Joe had us wait by the horse trailers when they arrived to send back the ones we thought were too sick. If we could fit a dime between its protruding ribs we wouldn't let it off the trailer. The ones we kept had to spend two weeks being retrained by the wrangler girls.

So when a wrangler called first thing in the morning from the stable and said an old horse had died, Joe said, "You fellas misjudged one," and we had to go out in the rain to dispose of the dead horse before the campers saw it.

Joe drove us to the pasture. The pasture ran along an incline with a large cup of earth surrounded by lodgepole pines with rainwater pooling over the roots. My coworker Kurt said that later in the summer the rain washes away the topsoil down to the clay, "and the clay gets slicker than snot."

Kurt and I took the tractor into the pasture. It was slow going—the wheels hardly caught in the mud. In the trees lay a dark brown quarter horse. Its head sloped downward enough to show a row of yellow headstone-shaped teeth embedded in the gums. Its unfurled tongue lay on the ground like a dull pink ladle.

"We'd be better off letting the mud swallow the damn thing," Kurt yelled over the engine noise.

The other horses were in the open part of the pasture. But the one they called "All-But" watched us through the trees. "All-But" had everything but one eye. The eye he had was a piercing cloudy blue. That blue eye was on us as Kurt tied a sheepshank knot to bind the dead horse's back legs together. He hooked a chain to the knotted rope and looped the chain on the back of the tractor where I stood as Kurt drove. He eased the tractor forward slowly so he wouldn't tear off the legs. When the chain was taut, he leaned on the gas, and the old horse pivoted from the pot of earth it died in. Once we got it out of the trees it slid easily over the wet mud. As it dragged over jagged rocks, I noticed chunks of the hide and meaty patches of the horse's side were left behind it. Joe held the gate open for us so none of the other horses could get out.

"Drag it as far into the woods as you can, and toss some brush cover over it," Joe said. He had on a mesh baseball cap and the beads of rain ran down the back of his neck. The cold did nothing to change his posture or his directness. He seemed like he'd done everything a hundred times. I admired this about him. Kurt drove past the horse barn, toward the woods, away from the little girls' cabins.

We untied it in the woods at the end of the camp's property. The hide had been scraped raw, and the last ten yards of mud we moved it through were blood-smeared. This high up, there was too much bedrock to bury it, so we used jigsaws to cut away at the surrounding trees' lowest branches and piled them over the horse until we could no longer see how mangled it was. Part of me felt we should have lit the pile on fire.

I rode on the back of the tractor as we returned the way we came. The rain washed the copper-red blood marks and clumps of horse hair away from the trail. There were already turkey vultures flying in wide spirals above the slope we left the horse on, the black finger of their beaks tracing the mountainside. The birds cut through the sky like they were scrolling something on the mountain's thermal updrafts—a language of nature's precision, its cycles of wind, that I was hoping would tell me how to start my life over.

The rattlesnakes on the mountain hide in the tall buffalo grass. When Joe hired me, he told me I was to kill them with a shovel and bury the heads right away. "Heads still bite," he said. "Them things probably won't kill you, but one of them little girls would be in real trouble. They don't have the bone density to deal with something like that."

Joe's from Oklahoma and he talked in short, slow clumps of dialect-ridden words I had a hard time understanding. His job came with a large house that sits off Dead Hawk Highway at the start of the ranch. His wife homeschooled their four beefy-looking kids. The kids followed us around when we worked in the barn. I'd seen the whole lot of them stand contentedly silent without talking for hours as we worked. It was actually comforting to be around, like they had something figured out that I hadn't yet.

Kurt is a master electrician who had worked on and off again with Joe for years. Kurt was in his midforties, had a sand-colored mustache and splotchy, beef-liver-colored cheeks. Joe told us what to do, and Kurt helped me do it right, half-jokingly calling me a "puny bitch of a man" every time I screwed something up.

"I'm from Cackalacky," Kurt told me when we first met. I had never heard the word, and he could see that on my face. "North Carolina," he said. When he gave me my first tour of the ranch, he showed me everywhere I could "take a dump."

He drove by a caravan full of campers pulling into one of the winterized group cabins. Skinny-legged girls piled out and started unsynchronized stretching routines before hauling out sleeping bags and plastic coolers. There was a mother barking orders while she patrolled the grounds where Kurt had shoveled and piled firewood. One of the little girls slipped on the ice and took a pretty bad fall. Kurt stopped the truck. He got out and helped the girl up. She smiled at something he said as he guided her over to the group mother. He was smiling as he got back into the truck.

"There's a few groups that visit in the winter. But most of the kids get dropped off in the summer on Friday afternoons by their parents and stay in the cabins for a week. They get marched around by camp counselors from activity to activity. Wait till summer. All you'll see is girls, girls, girls, in short-short-shorts. They all wear these little identical sashes, and believe me, they can break some shit. You'll be amazed at the damage those little girls can do, and we've got to go around fixing it. And here are the two rules you've got to follow: Knock and then pound on the door, yelling 'Maintenance' every time you have to go in a building so you don't get fired for walking in on them. You've got to do that even though you're there to fix clogged toilets and broken sinks, chase out bull snakes, or do whatever else you can to chase off the wilderness so they can play camper. And the biggest rule to abide by is one that I just broke: anywhere there are little girls, you better get your man berries somewhere else. We ruin the campground facade."

The three of us make up the whole work crew of the 750-acre ranch. We do the work to layer a nice face on a hard mountainside. The ranch used to be called Dead Hawk Ranch when an oilman used it for hunting, then he sold it to the Girl Scouts, who named it Bright Sky.

Kurt came to work every day wearing a mixture of brown or dull-green, sand-colored camouflage clothing. At first I thought he was some innocuous thug, but on his lunch breaks he studies Mandarin, which will be his seventh language. "I get that stuff," he told me. "Languages come easy to me."

Once, while we were eating lunch together I asked him what branch of the service he had been in.

"Contractor."

"Oh, you ran electricity for support buildings or something?"

"No, contracting—like soldiering. I was soldiering. I was an interpreter."

"When was the last time you were deployed?"

"A year ago."

"I bet you're happy to be away from that."

"I miss parts of it," he said. "Liked the work. Commute sucked."

"Where'd you get your military training from?"

"I'd rather not talk about that," Kurt said, and started slowly crunching on his chips.

His forearm had two dark blue bands tattooed into it. After a long beat of silence I asked him what the tattoos were all about.

"They mean something different to everyone," he said.

"Okay," I said. We ate again in silence. "You like it here, then?" I finally asked.

"Yeah. I like working outside. Doing something different all the time's nice too. I like seeing all these little girls having a great time. They get to have fun here. I like that. Seems important."

On an early June night Joe's truck horn woke me at three in the morning. I stumbled out of bed in time to see Kurt sprinting out of the truck and running toward my cabin. "Lewis. Lewis—wake up. One of the girls' cabins is on fire," he said. I put my pants, boots, and Buffalo Bills baseball cap on and ran outside with him and jumped in the back. As Joe pulled out of the driveway the truck tossed up a rooster tail of dirt rising behind us in the dark.

As Joe's truck got close to the crest of the hill, we could already see a giant plume of smoke towering upward. We were the first help to arrive and saw the camp director standing in front of a mountain of flames waving for us to hurry. A group of pajama-clad girls lingered in the trees in front of the burning cabin. Three counselors were each carrying a coughing little girl out of the front door.

Kurt ran toward them.

"We're missing one more," one of the counselors called to us.

Then one girl broke out of the back door of the burning cabin. Her nightgown had ignited from the bottom hem and flames rode up her backside, chewing at her hamstrings and lower back. The tips of her long hair curled up in red cinders and puffed into flame. She ran toward the back woods emitting this impossibly high-pitched primal scream.

The sound of her voice hummed in my bones.

Joe sprinted toward her, tackled her, and rolled over her to smother the fire beneath his body.

There was a little cloud of smoke around Joe's shoulders as he carried the girl to the field. "Get me some blankets," he yelled to us.

I ran into the next cabin, which had been evacuated, yelled, "Maintenance" out of habit, and pulled blankets off the first two empty bunks. When I got back to Joe, Kurt was staring at the burned girl. Joe and I wrapped the girl in the blankets. She didn't make a sound cradled in Joe's giant arms, but the smell of damp, burned skin made me dry heave. When the firefighters arrived I helped them find the hookups to the water systems for the fire engine.

The helicopter that arrived tilted its nose toward the high grasses to search for a place to put down that was clear of the treetops and fire's reach. It made about a dozen circular passes overhead.

"Land already," Joe yelled, as the helicopter tentatively descended between the dark trees. We loaded the burned girl into the helicopter. Then I watched it lift up and fade away in the dark valley below us, the red tail rotor light winking on and off until it curved behind a distant mountain. Joe and I loaded three other girls into ambulances. Kurt was standing in front of the husk of the cabin, watching it burn. The firefighters ran hoses so they were spraying the cabin from two sides, which began to taper the flames.

"Joe wants us to help get the rest of the girls settled for the night in the dining hall," I said, but he didn't move. "Kurt."

"The roof caved in, Lewis," he said.

"We have to go to the camping supply shed to get bedding for these girls," I said.

"I ran the wires for the lights in there. I ran them along the ceiling." He cupped his hands over his mouth and kept talking. "Jesus, I ran those wires." When I leaned in closer I heard that he was now talking in some other language, and I knew this sound and the smoke on the mountain would be in my dreams.

"Kurt, come on," I said, reaching my hand under his elbow to pull him away.

In the morning, Kurt walked into Joe's office with a snake's rattle in his hands. He lifted it up to us and shook it.

"You get one?" Joe asked.

Kurt shook the rattle again between his thumb and pointer finger.

"You don't look so good," Joe said.

Kurt tossed the rattle at me and I caught it before it hit my chest. In my open palm, it looked like the tiny stacked ringlets of a spinal column. Kurt looked like he hadn't blinked since we separated last night. "I laid the wires in that cabin," he said to Joe.

"I know." Joe stood up and walked toward Kurt and hugged him. "Nothing we can do about that," Joe said with his huge arms embracing Kurt. Kurt's arms were limp at his sides and he didn't make a move to hug Joe back or step away. He seemed disappointed in Joe's reaction, like he was hoping to be hit instead. "Let's work on what we can change," Joe said, as he let go of Kurt. "All right. I'm supposing we ought to make a showing of it at least." He waved us to follow him. The word *supposing* ran through my head. Kurt got in the passenger side, and I hopped in the back of the truck's four-door cab.

We drove to where the fire was. The early-morning fog still had a hint of smoke to it. Joe wanted me to mow a helicopter landing pad in the center of the field, where we'd make a circle of light to illuminate a ring on the dark mountainside for helicopters if anything like this ever happened again. He had Kurt calculate the amount of wattage we needed for the lights. Kurt had a little journalist notepad that he used to figure out the math. He kept referring to a phonebook-size electrician's chart and the Grainger catalog he kept in the back of the truck to match up what parts we needed. Of course, this planning was all too late. That one little girl was already in the hospital in Cheyenne getting breath pushed into her lungs by a machine.

The two of them left me to clear the field while they went to the hardware store to get the lights and cables. As I got all my equipment I imagined the eyes of bugs and squirrels and kestrels in the woods last night watching the fiercely glowing flame, their eyes reflecting the light. They would have been perched on what one of the books in my cabin—*The Alpine Arborist*—classified as Douglas firs, Rocky Mountain junipers, quaking aspens, lodgepoles, and pond pines. Some of these trees were "serotinous," meaning they require fire to open their seeds, which fall to the burned ground and start renewing everything.

I was pickaxing a six-inch-deep trench to run the wire when a shard of rock shot up and grazed my left eye. I covered that eye with my hand and walked to the mess hall bathrooms with the mirrors to see if I was okay. The little girls who'd been displaced by the fire were all still in their sleeping bags sprawled out on the floor. They'd all seen their friend on fire, and as much as I worried for the little girl in the hospital, I worried for these girls too. I knew it took only one small thing to fuck a little kid up, and then they have to spend the rest of their lives trying to move past it. One girl, still in her sleeping bag, watched me with my hand over my eye. I imagined she'd tell her friends my name was "All But."

I knocked on the bathroom door and said, "Maintenance" six times. I bent my neck to get a closer look at my face in the mirror. The microfiber-size capillaries stretched out like a vascular system, and the white of my left eye had a splattered egg-shaped bruise mark that I suddenly wished would spread, shadowing any lasting image of the burning girl from my mind.

When I walked back past the girls I held a wet paper cloth over my eye. On the trail back to the burned cabin I found giant padded footprints. Each was the size of a cantaloupe with dark holes where the nails sank into the dirt. A book in my cabin—*Large Mammals of North America*—talked about how avalanches in the winter catch unsuspecting animals like deer, and preserve them in the snow until spring, when bears wake up from hibernation to find the refrigerator at the base of the mountain fully stocked. It's a small little cycle that provides calories when they're most needed. The book also said that after spring, the black bear tends to wander farther and farther looking for food sources. I wanted Joe and Kurt to be back so I could show them the prints. I knew the burning smell from the cabin fire brought the bear, and the phrase *food sources* ran through my head.

After his investigation, the state's fire marshal told us that a faulty wire connection in the overhead lights had sparked. The sparks fell into the rubber trash bin full of paper towels, which ignited and filled the main room with smoke before flames crept along the wall and filled the bunk room. Kurt was next to me when we found out. I saw him swallowing some crushed expression on his face but he stood there as if he'd already accepted the blame.

The investigator told us that the girl was still in critical condition in the burn unit.

Joe told us the girl's family attorney had already contacted the Girl Scouts of the United States, and they might try to force the ranch to close.

A day after the fire marshal finished his investigation, we started tearing down the remnants of the burned cabin. We used the auger drill on the back of the tractor to unearth the floor beams and baseboards so we could plow them away.

"Y'all be careful with that thing," Joe said. I could tell he knew how hungover Kurt was. "I saw a guy get killed by getting caught in one of them and it ripped his balls off," Joe said to make sure we paid attention.

That night, I couldn't stop thinking about the wounded girl in the hospital. Her injury felt in some way connected to all the other hurts in my life, layering up like they do, with each new layer making you feel everything again, all the way down to the first hurt. Everything that had led me to be here in the middle of the mountains. My mother. My father. My brother and sister struggling to make their own paths. I got out of bed, but seeing how small and empty my cabin was didn't make things any better. In moments like this, I had a very hard time finding anything to look forward to, and I could only wait this feeling out until morning, when I watched the sunlight gush up the mountains, and tried to memorize the contours of every jagged stone.

A month later, on a hot July day, Kurt and I went to the western border of the property to clear some of the horse trails. In the John Deere Gator we drove by a group of girls walking single file down the road between two counselors. They all turned their backs to us so the truck wouldn't throw dirt in their faces, and as we passed them I saw how the sun caught in their hair. After we passed, Kurt leaned in close to me and sung a few guttural lyrics of a sad-sounding song that I couldn't understand.

"That's Farsi," he said. Then he got real quiet. "I feel sick about that fire," he said, breaking our unwritten code of not talking about it.

I leaned in closer so I could hear what he wanted to say. "Are you okay?" I asked him.

"This is real life up here. It's the true ugly and the high lovely." Kurt lifted and dropped his sunglasses off his eyes, and mumbled something again in some other language.

"The beetles kill a tree in about five years," Kurt said, changing the subject. "They suck the sap out from the inside like parasites." I looked around us on the trail. It was one of the most beautiful places I'd ever been in my life. The forested hillside was quiet too, with only those noises the mountain makes—rocks sigh, trees groan. Kurt didn't seem interested in talking anymore. It was quiet until we dragged out the chainsaw and started cutting down trees, already dead from Russian pine beetles, that were in danger of falling on the trail.

The tree trunks snapped off where they'd been cut at the base. There was a moment, when the saw stopped as the tree was falling, that things were completely silent again. Then branches drove into the dirt and snapped off before the tree crashed and the thud shook under our boots.

I cut down a few trees the way Kurt showed me, cutting a wedge from the opposite side I wanted it to fall before cutting across the trunk. I counted 118 rings on one of the trunks.

The woods we drove through were so beautiful. Each tree was full of amber-yellow light that I felt sink into me—like warm amber beetles that then slowly drained everything away, making me feel lighter as Kurt drove on.

In early August, Kurt offered to take me out one night. He drove us down Dead Hawk Highway to old Route 287 and over to Laramie. The fog was so bad we had zero visibility. Kurt let a semi go ahead of us, so he could follow the red strip lights of its trailer, and creep ahead until the semi took another route closer to the city. In Laramie the heavy fog bank lifted over the foothills so we could see the windmill farms, train tracks, and refineries. There were little tin-can trailers tucked into the rows of other tin-can trailers. The oil field owners held the deeds to most of them and rented them to the workers. From the road, the whole trailer park looked like a giant aluminum graveyard. Every bend off the road led to places like this, where people made lives which were, to me, completely foreign and unreachable, yet which I longed to know—as if living a moment of each, strange and lovely, would be the only way to know the world.

I was excited to be getting off the mountain. I had spent my nights waiting for morning, smashing golf balls off the deck, into the field, or shooting arrows at the plastic deer I set against a few hay bales off to the side of my cabin. Other than that, I read. I can't explain how desperate for any sort of significant human contact this left me.

Kurt parked the truck next to a few dozen other trucks in a parking lot behind a bar and turned the engine off without saying anything. He had his heavy boots and a pair of formfitting Carhartt pants on.

"This bar no longer has a door," Kurt said, and pointed to the entrance. "It's been broken so many times they put up a slab of particle board on the hinges instead. The board has the last names of everyone who can't come back inside. All banned for getting drunk and fighting."

"What's your last name?" I asked.

"Don't worry about that."

He didn't say a word as we walked into the bar, but I watched him closely anyway. He had a heavy jaw like a giant dog, and his upper body was hard, and his forearms were deeply tanned with their two blue rings. He was the indistinct sort that if you saw across the street you wouldn't wonder anything about his life. Though when he was close to you and you saw that his eyes were like the holes at the end of pistols, you snapped to some sort of alertness in his presence.

Inside, Kurt sat down and started ordering Seagram's 7 whiskey shots, drinking one after the other until he was talking loudly, mumbling in other languages. He then started trying to pick a fight with every man up and down the bar. He got several whipped up enough that they shouted at him like excited monsters, but no one would take him up on his offer, and again, that look of disappointment seemed to wash over him as he stumbled through the rest of the evening.

I tried to cajole him away from trouble until three men finally had enough and dragged drunken Kurt out of the bar and tossed him onto the gravel where he couldn't stand on his own. This made him scream, "You bastard!" over and over. I wanted to tell the three men that something important in Kurt had grown cancerous, and though I couldn't be sure, it may be contagious.

"That's one crazy SOB," one of the men said, but without any real shock or reverence for the whimpering rage they'd just seen. They struck me as very hard, old children.

Kurt called me a bastard as I helped him off the ground, and this made me want to scream in his face—*You drunken man-baby, look how ridiculous you are*. I shoved his shoulder to move him toward the truck, which made me feel strong, powerful, but he spun on me and pushed me away so hard I fell onto the gravel. Back in the truck I became fully aware he invited me here so I could drive him home. It made me feel foolish for thinking he was being kind to me. By the time I made peace with that fact, we were already working our way out of Laramie. When I got toward the highway Kurt told me to pull off the road and go down a dirt path.

"*Here!*" he yelled, and looked at me like he was going to break my neck. I was suddenly very scared of him.

I turned off the main road and drove through the woods. "I fish here," Kurt mumble-yelled to me. As we rocked over a dirt path on the way to the river, Kurt made whimpering sounds every time we hit a pothole.

"You sure you're not going to die on me, now?" I asked Kurt. He jawed away our whole drive from Laramie. Words came easy to him. But I couldn't imagine telling anyone about this—about the stories I was collecting in the west. I really couldn't think of anyone to tell. I parked where the wooded dirt road opened up to the exposed bank of the Laramie River. I walked upstream and stripped down so I was wearing only my boxers and walked into the river. When I leaned into the current, the water rolled off the slope of my shoulders and my limbs quickly went numb from the cold. The only thing I could hear was the rush of water pushing against me. When I lifted my head Kurt was in his underwear and walking into the river. Both of his legs were sleeved in totemic clan tattoos. There seemed to be no awareness of guilt in him for his earlier behavior. He was just a man walking into the water to clean himself off. I looked away. I dunked my head under again, and I wanted the river to rise higher and take me away, rise higher yet and take us all.

I had an even worse time sleeping after our trip to Laramie. I found myself on my deck watching the stars late at night. I watched the girls sneak through the field. I silently watched over them, as if proving something to myself, that I had some task here, as if that was all I really needed to feel fully alive. There had already been hundreds of little girls who'd passed through the camp since the fire, and each night, before I slept, I swore, I could hear them all. They had all left something of themselves on the mountain. I was happy for that too, knowing that on the outskirts of the ranch lay the chaos of their daily lives, filled with obligations and restraints of youth. Here, they ran free, and it was now my job to help keep whatever was waiting for them up the mountain away.

One night I could see that there was a campfire a mile behind my cabin. Stepping off my deck I smelled the wood and ash on the air. A group of girls was singing up there. The sound hit me like a secret, rich and sweet. I listened until they were quiet. Then the mountain noises took over. There were creatures snapping the twigs in the underbrush. This high up, there were tree frogs and cicadas that clicked at each other all night. Even the wind had a voice. In the darkness, I imagined the wind curling around like a banner floating in space. The image let me know how cyclical and tightly wound the natural world was, such that everything provided for everything else. And I knew the mountain itself was a book about those cycles.

I stepped off the deck and wandered into the forest. The sky was marbled by clouds covering the moon. There was an orange flush of campfire light through the trees. I walked toward the site as if it were all I ever wanted, a peaceful place to recover from my life so far. Then I heard the large snap of a branch behind me.

Some fear I hadn't felt in a long time slithered link by link up my spine, and I turned to see whatever it was.

Whatever was coming through the trees stopped in the darkness. I shut my eyes, and said nothing, hoping that this, finally, would be the right language to use.

In the hard darkness just below the tree line, I waited for a giant bear, the burning camper, or the bones of the dead horse with its head swaying toward its feet in that odd, broken angle. I could see them all, and searched for any words to let whatever was coming know I was there.

"Who's there?"

"Well—I'm supposing it's just a man from Cackalacky," the darkness said back. I saw a flash of his camouflage fatigues before Kurt moved away from me, this fellow man, hungry as the animals, starving for some labor to make him feel alive again. He wandered off into the gray—where in the evening and beyond, there is only a loose interpretation of how we should go about living.

I turned eighteen later that summer. And as the last of the Girl Scouts packed their bags for the season, I decided to do the same. I had caught the tail end of the mountain winter and did not want to weather a whole one. Joe had Kurt drive me to Cheyenne after a last day of working. Kurt wore his large black rubber-heeled motorcycle boots and drove too fast on the mountain turns.

I was relieved when the mountains leveled out and there were no more hairpin turns. Kurt drove even faster where the road bobbed up and down along cattle-grazing country. A dome of stars blanketed the sky. Just beyond the front range, Kurt stopped the truck and we both got out and climbed onto the roof. He had his binoculars and scanned the darkness and stars overhead.

"Not much of a telescope, but you can see a bit closer with these."

I scanned the night sky above the full sprawl of the north-westernmost Great Plains. The stars felt so low and bright that I could run my finger under them like a wind chime.

When he reached for the binoculars I caught a glimpse of his blue tattoo bands in the dark.

We stood there for a long time gazing up at the endless night sky.

When he turned the truck back on the road he pressed his heavy boot into the accelerator and we started gaining speed. He leaned forward as if he had a stiff back.

"You're going pretty fast," I said when I looked over and saw he was doing ninety miles an hour.

His foot eased off the gas. When I saw we had slowed down to eighty-five, I looked at the road and saw the outline of a black shorthorn cow twenty feet ahead and filling our lane. Kurt yanked the wheel to the right where the tires ground over gravel and our lights shone directly in front of us on another giant shorthorn that must have broken through the wire fence. Kurt heaved the wheel to the left, and back on the road between the two cows.

"Jeeeesus," I said, looking back to see the outline of those two cows disappearing. Kurt hunched forward farther with both hands on the wheels, looking ahead, a nervous half smile forming on his face. When I looked at him, I saw he was happy with his evening. With constructing some new hero's story of his life, what it was like to be set loose from whatever craziness he'd been through. Loose enough to find some new personalized foolishness that felt like living. He had somehow pulled me into his orbit. Driving with him that night, my feelings oscillated between sorrow for the difficult life he was probably bound to lead, and envy for his wildly beating heart, panicked, and fully alive.

Here I was, out in a strange place caught between the two separate worlds of my parents, and feeling that I was supposed to be a part of this third option that included wandering out on my own, far from any place I'd ever known.

Kurt took me to the Motel 6 that I'd cowered in before Joe brought me to the ranch months earlier. We parted with a brief handshake, which felt both anticlimactic and how men like him were supposed to communicate. Alone, in the dark parking lot the neon 6 sign seemed brighter than all the stars out on the plains combined. I paid for a room for the night. Once inside, I dropped my bag on the floor, took out the only set of enlistment papers I had left. The navy. I began to fill them out. I signed my name. *Lewis Thurber.* I placed the papers on the nightstand, ready for when the local recruitment office opened in the morning. Then I lay in the queen-size bed imagining spending the rest of my life letting my fingers graze the belly of every star in the sky.

6

Jamie Thurber, 1992

When we dropped out of the mountains heading west into Utah, we drove by one of those brown tourist attraction signs that read "The Trail Through Time," and I grabbed John's forearm so he'd read it as well.

"That might get us there quicker," he said, reaching over and squeezing his thumb and pointer finger above my kneecap where he knows it makes me jump. I planted my hands over his to hold it for as long as I could.

"Then we'd miss all this scenery," I said. There were carmine- and crimson-inflamed mesas stretching north and south of us; just ahead the road cut through the full spectrum of brown desert. It surprised me he'd wanted to make the trip, but working on his Jeep had been the only thing he'd wanted to do over the last four months, since getting back from the hospital in Italy. He'd marked the dates of Jeep Safari Week on the calendar like its arrival would heal him, and watched the highway ahead of us with the intensity of someone who had convinced himself that the road he was on would lead to a better place.

"The little specks of human cells that cluster up to make your eyes blue," I said to John. "How does that work?"

"That's a good one. I don't know," he said, obviously not in the mood to talk much more. The wind from our open top shifted the shortened bristles of his hair. On our road trips, I made him pick a topic for us to discuss in every way we could think of. I'd learned the trick from his mother, and hoped playing this game on our drive would crack something loose in him. John had chosen the color blue when we left Buffalo, but it looked like it was up to me to come up with the instances and meaning of how that color affected our lives.

I reached over and tried to run my hand up his leg toward his zipper, but he pushed it away. He kept looking at the road. "Are you okay?" I asked him.

"I'm fine," he said. That had become his mantra since getting back. It made me want to scream in his face. But I was afraid to push it with him. I wanted him to tell me he wasn't fine, so that together we could find the person he had been.

I kept one hand holding his on my knee and pulled out his dog tags from under my shirt with the other. I read them aloud, which was something I had been doing around him, as if trying to convince myself he was the same person. "Lieutenant, Junior Grade, Thomas John Parks. Naval Station, Newport, Rhode Island."

"Reporting for duty, Miss Jamie," he said, pulling the hand that had been on my leg free to salute.

We had dated all the way through college, and married a few years after graduating from Buffalo State, where I studied philosophy, music, and painting, and John did Navy ROTC to pay for school and please his veteran father. We spent the month after our wedding and before his first deployment in a California king-size bed his parents bought us for a wedding gift.

"Why do you love me?" I asked him in that bed.

"Because you have a gypsy smile," he said.

"What does that mean?"

"It's the kind where there's only one thing to do when you see it, completely abandon everything and blissfully follow."

We made love, and when he sat up I straddled him and buried my head into his shoulder, letting my hair fall forward over his back. When we finished I stood and pulled him up by the hands so we were facing each other.

"I want to look at you—at every part of you," I told him. "Move your body around. Flex for me and show me everything."

"This is everything," he said, standing in front of me. He was still breathing heavy and his penis was starting to slag back down.

"I mean it. Watch," I said. "I'll do it for you." I started breathing deeply, then shallow, and every other way I could manage. "See how my stomach folds a bit when I bend like this."

"*Let it all hang out,*" he sang.

"I'm serious," I said, kicking his blue-checkered boxers off the floor, toward him. "I feel fat when I do that. I have poses that make me feel sad, sexy, mean, and ugly too. I want you to show me all of you so I have more of you to think about when you're gone."

After I said that, he raised his arms over his head, flexing his fingers up to the ceiling so I saw the exposed stack of his rib cage.

He turned around with his arms still in the air and took a long inhale. I studied his body from the back of his neck to the muscles between his shoulder blades. He'd just finished recruit training at the Great Lakes Naval Service Training Command and was as lean and strong as I'd ever seen him, and for all my want to touch him again, I only watched as he moved for me until it was my turn, and I did the same. That's when he put his dog tags around my neck. They smelled like freshly minted nickel and chlorine. They were still warm from resting against his chest.

I wore those tags every time he deployed, and hadn't been able to take them off by the time we went to Utah. The tags also made me think of my brother Lewis, who traveled to distant ports, following whatever inner pressure urged him into the service. I held the tags in my hand every time I got a letter from John or talked to him on the phone, like they were an engraved promise that he'd be home soon. After he got hurt last October, when his ship was suicide-bombed in the port of Aden, I wore the sheen clear off the metal by rubbing them between my fingertips.

I'd heard about the bombing on the news before the navy recruiter showed up to our apartment. I saw his pressed black regalia through the peephole. He must have heard me gasp "No," before I dropped on the ground on my side of the door. I was scratching at the carpet with my fingertips like a dog when he knocked again, his sullen voice finding me through the doorframe. "Ma'am?"

I was sure the recruiter was there to tell me John was dead, but he pushed open the door and told me the blast had killed seven sailors, and wounded twenty-eight others. The explosion had torn open the right side of John's body from the quadriceps to lower rib cage. When they stabilized him, he was sent to the USS *Comfort* in the Gulf, then to a hospital in Italy where the doctors removed the eleventh and twelfth floating ribs on that side and grafted skin over the whole area.

We drove farther into Utah on I-70 and took Route 128 through the canyon leading into Moab. Our campsite was tucked below the road on the banks of the Colorado River, where the terracotta canyon walls rose a thousand feet on both sides of the water. "I love it here," I told John, as he pulled our gear out of the back of his Jeep to set up our tent along the river. The sun crossing from one end of the canyon top to the other shifted the shadows and changed the color of the walls and water. John stood by the river and tossed rocks—each plunking under the surface. He dusted the dirt off his hands by slapping them against his pants.

I unrolled our sleeping bags in the tent and lay down for a moment. The top of the tent was dusty, and I reached up and rubbed a squiggly line with my fingertip. The dust drifted down on me and I remembered how my mom went out the same night I learned about the Sistine Chapel in school as a girl and came back with a paper sack full of brushes and paints for me. She laid a drop cloth down in my bedroom, pulled a sheet taut underneath my box spring, and we lifted my bed onto four cinder blocks so I could slide beneath it and have my own canvas overhead.

"Give it a try," she said.

I lay on my back but didn't know what to paint.

"Whatever you like," she said. "Even if it is just colors."

So I started with a red daub on the white cloth. A drop of blood in a glass of water. Then I kept on without knowing what was to come and let the paint drip down onto me like a heavy rain.

When our campsite was all set up, we drove to town. I offered John some of my candy, Mamba fruit chews that I ate way too many of. In town, the streets were full of Jeeps souped-up in every way like I'd seen in John's Jeep magazines. He bought the Jeep for himself between his first and second cruise enlistments. He kept telling me to look at all the shocks, wheels, and roll bars on each one we passed. He got all excited and marched ahead of me so I noticed that each time his right foot came down his side pinched tight around his injury and his body hunched in on itself.

I wanted to touch his side to feel how his torso was tightening and releasing as he walked, though he hadn't so much as let me see him naked since he'd been home. We'd made love only once since he'd been back. He'd kept all his clothes on, slipping himself free of the open front of his Buffalo Bills boxer shorts. As he slowly started getting harder inside of me I brought my arms up from behind my head and softly pressed my hand over his right side. I put pressure against the gravelly texture of his scar tissue and felt the dip where his lower ribs had been—then he pulled away from me. "Please," I said reaching for John, trying to pull back all that want we'd worked up.

"No," he said, and left me there on the bed. When he left the room, all that love and longing I had for him when he was away and how scared I was when I couldn't visit him in far-off hospitals, rose up again inside of me and pushed against my skin. Since then, every morning, he'd take his tightly folded clothes into the bathroom with him and come out dressed after he showered. There was the mystery of how different he looked growing between us, and again, I kept silent.

We got trail maps at the visitor center, and walked through a couple of stores where John bought me an aqua-colored Jeep Week T-shirt, and himself a large window sticker that said "Feed the Rat," in bold white letters.

"What does that mean?" I asked him.

"It's a company that does all sorts of adventure-sports stuff. Get off on what you're into, is the idea. Keep the rat that's nibbling away at your insides happy by doing what you want." He pinched my shoulder and scrunched his nose up when he told me that, and I felt myself relax because he had touched me.

We walked down the street and passed an old movie theater that had been renovated for the tourists. I looked in through the enormous lobby windows and saw a wooden piano at the base of the movie screen. To sit at the base of a silent screen playing as the world came at you seemed magical to me.

"That's what I want to do," I told John.

"Well, you've got to feed the rat," he said, turning back to the line of Jeeps on the street. "Should we hit the trails?"

It was past dark when we got to the trailhead outside of Arches National Park. John walked to the Jeep and put his sticker on the windshield. He got into the front seat with two cases that he'd stolen from his unit and handed one to me. The box read "AN/PVS-7 generation 3, US Military Night-Vision Goggles."

He'd shown me how to use them after he got home from Italy, but I'd never put them on outside of our apartment. While I was taking mine out of the box I looked over and saw he already had his strapped around his head. The two eye pieces held by the head strap funneled into one eye lens like some sort of robot Cyclops.

Driving again on a dirt road, the night looked green and dull black through the goggles as we started down the trail. Lights from other Jeeps off-roading against distant hillsides resembled moon rovers, small and faraway, rocking over and through the same exposed stone that we were. We went about fifteen miles in, over mostly flat stretches.

"This is great," John yelled once, so I would hear, as if convincing himself he'd been cut free from the silence and weight he'd been holding. At the end of a long straightaway, he turned up a narrow slope with steep cutbacks. On sharp turns into the mountainside, the beams of our headlights shot out into nothing and dissipated in the distance.

The Jeep's front left tire suddenly slipped off the trail. My side of the car lifted and I could see straight over John's head and off the side of a cliff.

"Oh God!" John moaned. I wanted to squeal but could not. Panicked words were twitching in my mouth but nothing came out. John hunched over the steering wheel with his elbows jutted out, locked at ninety-degree angles, as he yanked the steering wheel toward me, slammed the gas pedal, and the Jeep straightened on the trail again. The long muscles in his forearm were taut as piano wires.

John continued along the switchback ridge as slow as he

could go without having the car roll backward. From my seat, I watched the cup of a valley sinking below us again.

At the top of the hill, he stopped and set the parking brake. He was pale, and sweat beaded at his forehead. We sat there for what felt like hours—each in our own state of paralysis—frozen from the gut out, silent again beneath the moon.

"This is a pretty serious grade going down," he finally said. I scanned the area and realized there was no room to turn around. The pale green moonlight lay on the hillside like a mesh blanket over the trees. "Do you want to drive?" he asked me.

"Are you crazy?"

"I'm serious," he said, looking at the path leading down. "I'll put it in a low gear and walk in front of the Jeep telling you how to position the wheels."

"Why don't I tell you where to go?" I asked him.

"Well, I think putting the Jeep where I tell you will be better than you guessing where it should go." From the exposed part of his face below the goggles, I saw he was chewing the inside of his cheek hard enough that I'm sure he tasted the tang of blood mixing with spit. He'd let me drive the Jeep around town, and a few times on trails near our apartment—but never like this.

"Please—no," I said.

"Please!" he said, and I wondered again at what inner trouble he was fighting.

"This was the kind of thing you've been talking about doing since getting the Jeep."

John started making coin-size circles against his jeans pocket with his right pointer finger.

"Yeah. But—but this is a complex route down."

"And you want me to do it?" Through the green darkness of my goggles, he didn't look like anyone I'd seen before, and for the first time since he'd been back I was genuinely afraid I'd lost the man I once knew. It sickened me, but part of me longed to go back to the carpet floor with the recruiter's voice in my ear. If only a bit more fire had flashed into the side of his ship, I could have mourned him, and gotten on with my life. What kind of wife thinks this? I was a monster.

He got out of the car and walked away from me. His limp seemed exaggerated on the dirt road.

"I don't know why you can't do this," I said, terrified of the descent around us on every side.

"I'll walk you through," he said, turning back toward me. "We'll be fine." I looked at him closely, and the goggles made it look like he was backlit by a neon glow.

"You'll tell me what to do?" I asked him.

"That's my girl," he said, leading me to the driver's side where he buckled me in and put the Jeep in its lowest gear. I kept my goggles on and looked for the spot on his body where his nerves had been rattled loose. He started walking ahead of me, pointing to where he wanted the left tire.

"Give it a little gas," he yelled, in a voice I'm sure platoons would listen to without question, but within which I knew something childish was trembling. He did this, bottled up all his hurts, as if words were insufficient for such things, and then I'd keep silent so as not to add to any of them. But the silence between us had turned gangrenous. I could feel it in my stomach.

When I hit the gas the left side of the Jeep climbed over a small boulder and my stomach tightened as I saw where the switchback dropped over the edge—where life collapsed toward a pile of unforgiving rock. This was the spine of the mountain, the slightest movement in the wrong direction, and the Jeep would have fallen—I would have fallen—fallen alone.

The tire rolled back down and I steered it from small stone to stone without listening for John. He may have stopped talking. When I looked up at him, his body was like a jiggling water balloon, sinking in on itself and disappearing. He was disappearing right in front of me, and instead of terror, what I felt under my skin, where I had kept all of my own hurt and loss and love, was a deep sense of release.

The trail wrapped around the side of the escarpment and narrowed again. I kept my foot buried into the brake pedal like it was my gravity. We inched down that hill taking dozens of switchbacks that evoked fiery crashes in my mind, until the steep grade finally leveled out and I pulled ahead of John, taking the turns by myself. When it finally flattened out I stopped.

John walked past me, ahead of the Jeep about thirty feet on the flat surface and kneeled on the ground like a limp ladder, his crunched profile fully lit by the headlights. I saw him reach up and push the goggles off his face, his outline trembling ahead of me—green, lit, deflated.

Sitting in the envelope of light coming from the Jeep, his buzzed hair looked like something with swaying bristles on the bottom of the ocean, light moving through it. His hands were shaking at his side until he brought them to his waist and unhooked his belt buckle, pulling it away from his body like a lawn mower cord. The leather belt snapped as it sprung out of the last belt loop. He kicked his sandals off and pushed his pants down around his ankles. He tripped sideways, lifting his legs out of his pants, but stepped right back into the center beam of the headlights. He brought both his hands to the neck hem of his T-shirt and pulled it over his head. He held the T-shirt in front of him—crumpled in his hands it looked like a massive raisin—and dropped it at his feet. Then he pushed his boxers down and stepped out of them—closer to me.

The image, I knew instantly, would be in my head forever—grotesque and terrible. It looked like a large shark had taken a mouthful from his midsection and now something hideous was climbing up his side. His torso was deeply road-rashed. The skin bubbled up and fused into discolored pink and white cords weaved together. The divot of his thigh muscle along the right quadriceps sunk close to the bone. His penis leaned to the left, as if trying to fall away from the monstrosity of his sheared body. If I were to paint him, I would have had to use a sponge to blotch and texture the wound. He spread his arms out to the side so his palms were facing me.

I kept facing him, even though all I wanted to do was turn away. I shut my eyes to the green light searching out the contours of his truth in the dark. I swatted at the side of the goggles looking for some button that would turn everything though the lenses black—or off. My hands gripped the steering wheel harder than they had on our descent, as if I were trying to cement myself to it, so I wouldn't have to touch anything else.

I got out of the Jeep and walked toward him.

I'm not sure why he chose that moment to tell me, or what specific fear had been conquered in the Jeep, but when I got to him, he looked up at me and said, "It was full of watermelons."

"What was?" I asked.

"When I got hurt. The little boat that exploded along the ship's hull and blew right under the crew-mess chow line. The explosion knocked me through a galley wall into a whole room jammed full of watermelons." His eyes were fixed on the road. "They had a whole room full of these pallets of watermelons that they were going to give to the crew at a picnic. I have no idea how they got so many over there, but that's what one of the rooms that got hit was full of. Watermelons. It was a piece of that galley wall that took out my ribs."

He made a hollow popping sound with his tongue as he knocked his fist against his right side.

"There was red pulp and seeds all over the deck and dripping down from the overhead," he sort of snorted out a laugh. "I never passed out either. For a second, I felt an unbelievable pain. Then I stopped feeling anything, and watched as things went to hell, sitting with all that fruit until someone gave me a shot of morphine."

He'd never told me anything more than what the recruiter who came to our apartment had. I knew he was hurt during a terrorist attack on a US naval ship, but that was all.

"Where'd they get all those watermelons from? I never stop thinking about them."

I listened to him talk and stared at his open side, raw like the punched rind of a watermelon. I imagined what John's scars would look like when he was older.

"It was so goddamn random," John said.

The sound of the land around us filled the night with slow rhythmic pulses.

"On the USS *Comfort* they kept me on a morphine drip. I kept waking up in these half-crazy stupors imagining I was loading up the ship's one-hundred-and-thirty-millimeter guns with watermelons and blasting those things all over the desert. I could actually see the seeds once they landed and scattered all over, dropping into those little crevices in the sand.

"I think I dreamed about watermelons growing in the desert the whole time I was in the hospital, my imagination trying to explain where they came from."

The glow from the headlights shifted our shadows on the hillside below us. He kept talking after we climbed back into the Jeep, but it was too much for me. I shut my eyes, letting my eyelids coat everything blue until it was all gone. I wanted to scream so loud that I'd silence John and even knock him down and blow him off the rocks. I wanted to be alone again, and I tried to imagine driving myself home. But even with my eyes shut, there he was beside me in the Jeep, the desert spreading out around us as we made our way back east; our topic for the return trip, not *blue* or anything so abstract, but the simple question of how we would go about "surviving together." As we crested the watershed of the Rockies to the east, we looked down on all that history we shared, all that history that sat there, waiting for our return.

7

Connor Thurber, 1995

The new house is a quarried-sandstone ranch built in the late fifties on a wooded acre with a serpentine creek cutting through the backyard. The great room has a pitched ceiling and three walls of high windows that flood the cherrywood floors with light. You and I loved it as soon as we went up the driveway. You liked the open, well-lit layout, and I liked how the lushness of the property made it seem like there were no neighbors. We both liked the idea of our son, Dennis, playing with his dog in the large yard, climbing trees, collecting pine cones, catching crayfish.

We offered pizza and wine to friends who helped us move, and by the end of the first day all the couches, love seats, and boxes were inside. We set up Dennis's room first so he'd have a comfortable place to sleep, but that night he slept in our bed anyway, a hot, wiggling creature kicking us awake. The curled dog twitched at the foot of the bed. After years of living in temporary condos without enough space, this felt like finally arriving at what we wanted.

Early the first morning a quick thumping sound wakes me. I ease the boy's arm off my shoulder and walk down the hall into the great room. Dust motes glow in the first orange rays of sunlight. The dog's nails *clack-clack-clack* behind me. I walk to the sliding door to let him into the backyard. Only 360 mortgage payments to go. Thirty years of our life here. Our son growing and us growing older. It's strange, scary, and overwhelming all at once. I walk from room to room looking for what made the noise, and it's nice to watch the light spilling across these new floors.

The dog scratches at the door. I let him in—*clack-clack-clack*—then stand studying the yard and the trees, the steeples of the Egyptian Coptic and Lutheran churches across the stream near the highway, until I hear a crunching from down the hall. The dog is gnawing on a bird in the center of the boy's room. Feathers and blood spread around his paws.

"No. No!" I yell, jumping for the dog, who is a gangly black-and-white Newfoundland puppy who mistakes this for play and dodges by me and runs into the hall, trailing black feathers. Before I corner the dog in the kitchen, he devours the rest of the bird—bones, feathers, feet.

"What? What?" I hear our son say from the hall.

The boy is looking at the masticated bird wing and all the blood in the center of his new room. He wears pajamas with teddy bears on them, and his stuffed rabbit hangs by the ears from his tiny hand. I scoop him up and palm the back of his head so he'll rest on my shoulder.

The next morning, another thump, like a piece of fruit hitting the floor. The dog gets up and runs to the door to be let out. I go out first and walk around the perimeter of the yard. The grass is wet and cool in the webbings of my bare feet. I pass the cracked patio that needs mud jacking to level the concrete and the rusted AC unit that needs replacing. I don't know how to do either task. At the base of one of the large windows is a dead grackle. I pick it up by the tip of its long tail feather and study the black pupil of its pale yellow eye. Its iridescent black neck hangs crooked. I carry it to the stream. The dog scratches at the glass door and wags its tail at the sight of the bird. At the stream's edge, I fling the bird into the fast-moving center and watch it float away on the surface before dipping under.

Another bird crashes into the window later in the day. This time, Dennis runs to the window, puts his forehead and hands against the pane, and looks down into the brush outside. When he looks at me, I notice the oil from his skin has left prints on the glass.

I give that bird to the stream, too.

Through the first week, enough birds crash into the glass that I take a five-gallon bucket and walk around the house collecting them in the morning before the dog is let out.

I read online that hanging CDs threaded by fishing line from the eaves can catch the sunlight and scare the birds away, so with a ladder I hang a dozen around the house.

"That looks so awful," you say. "What will the neighbors think? It looks like we're crazy people warding off evil spirits."

But the CDs help. Still, that first month the dog comes in with feathers sticking out of the corner of his mouth, and the thumping of something hitting the glass at high speed wakes me at dawn.

Then, on a Saturday morning, you call from the backyard. You're holding Dennis. He's crying and pointing to the ground.

"What? What?" Dennis says.

A mockingbird is doing circles on its side by thrashing a wing into the dirt. Its little chest is heaving. Dennis is ruddy with tear-glossed cheeks, and his hand opens and closes in an attempt to clutch the bird.

Perhaps it's because of our son watching, but I bend down and cup the bird's still-warm and delicate body in my hands. Both the bird's wings flitter against my fingers. I release my grip to see if it will fly, but it hops off and falls to the ground.

"No, Dada," Dennis wails.

A feeling of foolishness sweeps over me. That familiar wave of uneasiness descends out of the endless blue sky.

"That was smooth," you say.

Everything in me goes numb except for a hot, dark presence in the back corner of my mind, a place I try to avoid.

"What am I supposed to do?" I ask you.

"Let's take it inside and see if we can fix it. Let's at least try," you tell me.

For the next week, the bird lives in a cardboard box on the kitchen counter so the dog won't get it. Dennis peeks through the holes punched in the top and side, and every evening sprinkles seeds down to the bird.

Every morning, I wake to the bird singing at the first light, a long, trilling sound followed by high-pitched squeaks. The box is alive, and it's early when I sit next to it and imagine giving this animal to the river when no one else is around, but I admire the little bird's full-throated heave, how it jumps and tries to work its speckled wings.

Its morning song spreads through the airy house, gifting away the silence. I have seen every sunrise from the great room since moving in. The boxes are all unpacked. The paintings made and framed by my mother and sister as gifts are on the wall. The dog has established a routine of where to sleep throughout the day. There are 359 more payments to go, and I have to clean the chimneys, spray for mold in the crawl space, and work my way down an endless list of tasks you have written out for me, but there is this birdsong. Life in one place doesn't seem as scary as it had felt to me on that first morning. Time moves fast, and with the birdsong in the house, I am more aware of the rustle of living creatures. I look for the starlings, finches, jays, even squirrels. The sound of the stream babbling and the bullfrog's deep moans coming from the evening fog. Short-horned crickets. Tulips opening in the heat. The world is as new and alive to me as it surely is to our son. Newly opened fringes of discovery.

The Encarta disc suggests letting the rehabilitating bird wander on a string to get used to hopping and flying short distances after its neck or wings recover. The three of us go to the backyard and watch as the bird takes a few hops into the center of the yard. In the sunlight, the white-streaked, brown feathers are ablaze. Other birds sing in the trees. Then the little bird jumps up and flies halfway across the yard. The fishing line around its leg unspools and the boy laughs.

"Look at that," you say, and you do a fake little clap to get Dennis excited.

Then a hawk drops straight down on top of the rehabilitated bird and pins it to the ground between its talons. One reddish-brown wing stretched out shields the bird.

When the hawk flies upward, the fishing line pulls taut and becomes a living kite in my hands. It flies in tight circles above the yard, hovering like an apparition. I pull the line, and for every foot I take in, the hawk takes half a foot back. The fishing line falls in tangles at my feet and Dennis bends down and grabs the loose coils so the two of us are tethered to the hawk.

Dennis is doing a pained dance next to us, his body lithe with the discovery of its growing range, which is the deepest sort of beauty, and I feel all my love spilling down into our son as I pull the line in.

"What are you doing?" you yell at me.

"I don't know," I respond, and in that moment a surprising feeling sneaks up on me and I realize I mean that I don't know what I'm doing with the hawk, but also with the boy at our feet, with this house, and even with you. I mean for the statement to stand for all of this, and as I keep pulling, it feels I have confessed something I didn't know I was hiding.

When the hawk is a few feet over my head, it still hasn't let go of the mockingbird. The hawk thrashes as I hold the wild bird there like I'm Adam in the Garden, about to give the creature its new and eternal name. I reach for its legs, and the hawk strikes my forearm with its beak, breaking the skin. Then I let the line go; the hawk rises over my head and trails the fishing line, which unspools off the ground, through our little boy's grip, cutting its course over his soft pink palm and loosening a fine track of blood from the heel to the webbing. His little cry of pain cuts me in half. Only when the boy cries do I really notice he's holding the line too, and I see the last of the dangling teal thread slice from his grip and drift away.

I snatch up Dennis. You open his wounded palm and press one cuff of your shirtsleeve into the cut. With the cuff of your other sleeve, you squeeze the cut on my arm and we stand in our yard staunching the blood, listening to the birdsongs and the babble of the creek harmonizing, which now feels like the pulse of a world I might finally be coming to know.

8

Terrance Thurber, 2000

Terrance's accident made the local papers. He was working on a circuit breaker forty feet off the ground between the Chevrolet dealer's show lot and the Pizza Factory in Kalispell. He had re-routed the power grid so he could work on the local transformer. There was a checklist of things he'd gone through and marked with a red Bic pen before he climbed the steel ladder to the high retention wires. He had done everything right too. Alberta-Montana Power Company would check it all several times afterward. It was someone at the main power switchboard, thinking that the diversion was a mistake, who put it back to its normal current flow. Terrance had already started working when the power was sent back toward him. He heard a humming. It got louder, bigger, and the few fine hairs above his knuckles on his right hand stood straight up before everything crested into him.

He felt as if he'd been sliced into millions of thin biopsy cuts that rattled against each other, until everything inside his body pushed against everything on the outside. His eyes bulged like overfilled balloons, and his world went teal blue—then red from his blood rushing to his head as he hung upside down from a harness. Then everything went black when he passed out.

The head of his hammer pressing against the outside of his lower thigh got so hot it burned the shape of itself through his thermal Carhartt pants and into his skin. The dealership filed a claim because his screwdriver shot fifty feet out of his tool belt and punctured the passenger-side door of a new gunmetal-gray Tahoe truck in the lot. A witness was quoted in the *Hungry Horse News*, saying he looked like an "epileptic fish flopping above the road."

He wasn't sure for how long, but for a while before he woke up, he was conscious of who he was but not of his body. He felt the bones in the top of his right foot first. They were floating there by themselves like the bare spines of a Chinese hand fan. Then he felt how those bones connected to his ankle, and there was only his one foot. He felt it wholly, as if it supported the weight of the world like Atlas. When he started to think about his leg, his shinbone ached, then his knee. In this way, as if he were the God of himself, creating one small piece at a time, he reassembled his body until he became aware of being in the hospital bed. He felt holy. Except for the sharp pain in his groin, gravity did not apply to him, and he was ascending to something.

The room was empty when he woke. His left leg was in a stirrup. It felt like something was resting on the outside of his skin—a teal-blue fear trying to get in—or the outer layer of himself had been burned off and everything was nerve-end sensitive.

Helen walked in five minutes later with a cup of coffee and a bag of yogurt-covered pretzels. She didn't look up at him until he asked, "Am I okay?"

She made a guttural *ugh* sound and dropped the coffee on the floor. The puffed-up, subtly bruise-colored skin under her eyes made them squinty, and she looked like a haggard version of herself. She had stopped sleeping several weeks before, after she'd lost her job as the secretary to a high school principal. For some reason, she had torn every sheet of paper she had filed away in half, and she could not answer Terrance's or the principal's questions about why she had done that.

When she dropped the coffee, Terrance wanted to touch her face the way a blind person would, with hungry fingers trying to find something. He wanted to push the stray strands of her bangs behind her ear, but all her hair fell loose as she leaned over the bed and sunk her face into his neck. Her highlighted brown hair covered his eyes. She stayed like that for a long time. "I thought you were going to die," she said. Then she pushed herself off him and ran out of the room to get a doctor.

Everything around Terrance felt lighter as a doctor told him about the half-dollar-size hole between the inside of his left thigh and testicles, where the current of electricity that entered his body had ripped out. Surgeons had sutured and skin-grafted the wound during the thirty-one hours he had been unconscious.

That feeling of lightness stayed with him the whole week he was in the hospital. The doctors kept him because they wanted to make sure nothing was wrong with the circulation of his femoral artery. He slept most of the week, waking each time with his mind fixated initially on the bones of his right foot and then working its way over his body, making sure everything was still there. When he wasn't sleeping he sketched his awakening skeletal system in his notebook and drew things he would carve once he was released.

"Did your life flash before your eyes?" Helen asked him while they were alone in the room together.

"No," he said. "There's too much of it to happen all in one little moment." She looked disappointed by his answer. He probably should have said something about thinking of her. He was worried about why she had been fired and how soon they could both get back to work. Maybe he should have mentioned something about Los Caporales, the Mexican restaurant off Highway 93 where they had met five years ago. She was thirty-seven at the time and had never been married. Terrance was fifty, and had been divorced for years. His ex-wife, Catrin, lived near Olean, New York, and they rarely talked. He wrote letters once a week to his three kids ever since he left New York. Since he left them. Jamie sometimes wrote back. Connor less frequently. Lewis never did. Not once. He didn't know where Lewis was. That was the price of a messy early life. Helen was the only one who visited him in the hospital; the rest were out there in a place he could not get back to. That alone seemed like it would be hard to condense into one brief flash before a person could die. So much to make peace with in one lifetime.

His cabin was on 160 acres of land in the Bitterroot mountain range. It sat against the foothills side of an expansive oval field that his grandfather had cut back into the surrounding woods when he first bought the land in 1938 for next to nothing. Terrance had made the cabin his year-round home after he moved back to Montana.

The first three days out of the hospital, Helen lifted his leg from the couch and rested it on her shoulder as she rubbed the salve he'd been given at the hospital on the burn scar on his crotch to keep the skin moist. On the fourth day, he had full range of motion back in his leg, and Helen helped him limp around the cabin the rest of the weekend. On that Monday, he drove himself to the office at Alberta-Montana, where his bosses and their lawyers were waiting to offer a settlement package to keep them out of court. They were willing to offer him a 2.3-million-dollar pension plan that would kick in next month. One million dollars spread out over eighteen years and 1.3 million paid in full at the end of that time. He felt a subtle wave of shock roll over his body like he was hanging upside down again. He imagined it was a similar feeling, from her descriptions, to Helen's orgasms.

Terrance signed the papers.

When he got home, Helen was under the covers on the couch with the salve cream cupped in her hands like a tiny bowling ball.

"I thought you had been killed," she said. "It would have been me—all alone." She lifted her body off the couch and hugged him. "I thought you had been killed."

Terrance sat next to the couch, and Helen's hand started clutching the hair on the back of his head. There was a buffalo skull that he'd cleaned and mounted above the fireplace. Two-track light bulbs illuminated it against the brick. The eye sockets of the bison skull were empty. He turned to Helen, and her eyes seemed just as exposed and vault-like. Something in her had come unlatched and was swinging around inside. He felt the shrill screech of an alarm sounding up his spine, as if his skin was still so very thin and offered no barrier between him and the world. All of this had happened before. Her moods had always swung between outrageously happy and a bone-tired funk that ushered her into the flatness of depression. The struggle with each had been exhausting, but now he wanted to once and for all mend it.

He pulled the blanket over her shoulders and rubbed his fingertips against her temple until she fell asleep. He didn't have to tell her about the money. She knew he'd receive workers' compensation checks until he wanted to go back to work, so he wouldn't have to tell her. Another one of those ghost currents shook through his body.

When Terrance woke up, his sketchbook was resting on his stomach—he'd been sketching another sculpture he now wanted to build—and he was on top of the covers. The room was dark. The alarm clock on the side of his bed read 1:13 A.M. The bright LCD screen shone on the floor. He closed his eyes and opened them to get the sleep out, then turned on his reading lamp.

There were chrome-oxide-green footprint outlines on the carpet leading into his room. His heart knotted like a fist when he saw where Helen's thin feet had lightly touched the ground as she came in. Next to his bed there was a mass of footprints, where she must have stood for a while. She had been watching him sleep again. He walked into the living room and found her rolling dollops of paint into the carpet with a roller brush. She had the five-gallon paint bucket from his work truck that he used for neighborhood circuit boxes. She'd either rolled the brush over her chest or lain in the wet paint, as there was an outline of the large cups of her bra highlighted in chrome-oxide-green on her shirt.

"Helen—"

The ends of her hair had sealed together in clumps, with paint. She had finger-painted the corners of her eyes as if she were accentuating the crow's-feet and now looked like a tired forty-something-year-old child.

"What are you doing?"

"I'm devastated," she said to him and bent forward over her lap so her forehead was resting on the carpet.

Terrance phoned the hospital after she fell back asleep. "Is she off her meds?" the doctor on call at the clinic asked.

"She swore she wasn't," he told the doctor, who said to keep an eye on her and bring her in that afternoon.

Terrance was wide awake from falling asleep so early. Helen's presence in their bed seemed to fill up the entire space of the cabin. He didn't know how he'd make it until morning, wondering how to help her. For the rest of that night, he pulled out the ruined carpet, cutting away at the corners and rolling it up at the center of the room. Enough paint had soaked through to dye the carpet glue green. He thumbed the green glue marks and hoped she had gone off her meds and it would be an easy fix.

She had gone to what they ended up calling a "therapy retreat" once since they'd moved in together. He had hoped she'd be able to address some central event of her life that she could then move on from. She came back with a small painting she had done from a flyer for a horse show. It was something completely out of the norm for her, but she kept it on the wall of the cabin. Terrance looked over at it as he took a break from pulling up the rug. It was a watercolor copy of a sequined woman standing on a galloping white horse. She wore a blank white mask with feathers that hid any part of her except her eyes, which were shadowed and dark. *Priscilla the Performer* was written in white paint across the bottom.

He had snuck one of her unmarked meds after she'd gotten back, to see what they did to a person. The next morning he'd had to call in to work for the first time. When he finally did get out of bed, it was with equal parts fear of how intense the drug was and how out of touch with his body it made him feel. He was also curious as to what chemical it was that kept Helen up and running. As he continued to pull up the rug now, all that fear returned, knotting between his shoulders.

A few days later, Terrance filled his nostrils with cotton swabs so he wouldn't smell the putrid meat scraps hanging off the buffalo skulls he'd gotten from the bison ranch. He coated the horns with a thick layer of Vaseline so the ants wouldn't eat away the enamel, and left the heads on anthills. The ants would clean away the tendons and tunnel to the marrow, if a bear or coyote didn't decide to come gnaw on it first. His grandfather had taught him how to clean bones like this when he was a boy. Then he piled the bones and antlers into a cargo net. He set the net in the deep part of the Kootenai River tributary on a rope he tied across the water so the current would bleach them smooth.

He'd been carving bones and antlers his whole life—making eagles, bears, wolves, and other "high Alpine art images." Danny, a friend, would sell them in his tourist store outside of Glacier National Park. The bones had added a lot of extra income over the years.

Now Terrance walked back through the snow to the cabin with a full elk rack over his shoulders. The hilt from the crown of the elk's head rested against the back of his neck, and the horns draped over his shoulders in front of him like a giant thorn scarf. He was thinking of the sculpture he wanted to build: how with the large bag of bones in the cargo net, he'd have everything he'd need.

He weaved out of the woods with the antlers and came into the open valley south of the cabin. The cabin had been a sanctuary for him since his divorce, giving him all the time he wanted to set out into the woods and mountains and collect his bones.

After Helen woke up he drove her north to Whitefish, where he dropped off a truck full of bone carvings to Danny's gift shop. Danny was in the store, wiping a dirty rag over a glass display case of turquoise jewelry. Helen helped Terrance unload the carvings. They took one at a time through the back door of the building to the storage area; there Danny would decide where he wanted to display Terrance's work.

"This one is lovely," Helen said as she pulled a length of elk horn out of the truck cab. Terrance had carved a series of figures running from the base toward the points. They showed an evolutionary progression, from a hunched-over Neanderthal to better and more upright hunters. The final figure was standing straight, with a bow drawn taut across his chest. Terrance had carved them using small bend gouges and skew knives. He'd often work on them late at night so Helen wouldn't be awake by herself. In the morning, he'd wake to her sweeping up the pittings off the floor.

When they finished unloading the truck, they drove south toward the clinic in Kalispell. The hospital was the first major development on a gigantic plot of land. For Sale signs advertised the other lots in the surrounding fields. At the clinic, Helen went into the doctor's examination room while Terrance walked around the building.

In the summer all that was in those fields were bleaching bones and weeds. Now the light off the snow made everything seem refrigerated. A yellow finch landed in front of him on a tall, dead blade of olive grass. The grass curved slightly under the bird, which dropped a little white splatter of shit and flew off. There was a frozen burlap seed sack stuck to the ground along the fence bordering the parking lot. Terrance pulled it up from the snow, and it tore grass out of the ground like a Band-Aid on arm hair. Camel crickets, potato bugs, and centipedes squirmed in the exposed earth.

His grandfather used to read the Bible to him. Terrance had been fascinated by the story where Jesus walked on water. Maybe it was having lived entrenched in this kind of earth and so far from any sea that made the whole matter an utter mystery. Terrance used to think about Jesus walking on the water and how fine a thing it must have been. Now he thought how Jesus must have walked from the water back onto land—back into this—and felt a bit of a letdown. He wondered if Jesus felt water underneath his feet for the rest of his life, the way Terrance suspected he'd feel a blue current running through him.

When he went back inside he read Oprah's magazine instead of a pamphlet called *On Living with People Who Suffer from Various Mental Disorders and Imbalances.* He had spent the last several years learning the clinical language of disorders and imbalances. He had been there with Helen through the course of trying to find the right balance of medications. He'd held his concerns in check as the medicines seemed to be getting stronger with each doctor's visit, cycling through anticonvulsants, before moving on to lithium and carbamazepine.

From the waiting room, he saw a doctor with his head down, writing and talking to Helen at the back counter. He tore a pharmaceutical script from the pad and handed it to her. She put it in her pocket. Terrance thought of setting her up somewhere other than the cabin when he got his settlement money.

"How'd it go?" he asked when she came out.

"Let's go," she said.

"Wait. Do we need to get your prescription filled?"

"Please, let's get out of here, Terrance." Her voice was limp. Something in her face looked crushed, and he couldn't bear keeping her there. They went to the truck, and he started driving her north to the cabin.

"Are you okay?" he asked Helen when they were driving.

"I need to be sad for a while," she told him as they drove.

"Why are you so sad?" he asked. She was looking out the window at the rolling fields.

"Terrance," she said, letting his name hang in the space between them. "I used to feel it."

He knew she was about to drop some hammer on him, something that had been festering. "Feel what?" he asked.

"I could feel my body wanting a baby. If I was around one, I could feel it in my bones." She turned away from him and looked out the window. "I stopped feeling it. It was this sort of pang. Something inside of me I couldn't explain, that got louder and louder when I got older. Now I can't hear it anymore. It stopped."

Terrance reached over and put his hand on her knee, but she pulled her leg away.

"We were never going to have a family. I was always too scared of having kids take after me to try." She was pressing herself into the doorjamb. "And—you—never pushed us to do it!" Her voice was full of anger, and she shot out and punched his arm as hard as she could.

His elbow buckled, and the truck veered to the side of the road for a moment, vibrating over the rumble strip and gravel before he pulled it back. Her eyes looked like the hollow buffalo's again.

"We're not going to have a family!" she screamed at him. Her sudden rage was unfurling in front of him, and something reckless was pushing out of her, making her glow.

"You'd probably be a shitty husband and a shitty father again anyway," she yelled, hitting him where she knew he was most vulnerable. "You're not even worried about me either, you just don't want to be stuck taking care of me forever."

Terrance was silent.

"Say something!" Helen yelled.

"Right now that's true. Right now I'm sick of you," Terrance blurted out.

"So what? Right now I hate you!" Helen screamed. She sounded vicious, and Terrance felt the dread that there would be no washing clean after something like this. There would just be plodding ahead, both of them worn to emotional shreds.

Helen hadn't taken her eyes off him. Everything dark and confusing in her was working its way through her stare into the side of his neck as he drove. There was too much to flash in front of a person's eyes before they died, all right, he was sure of it.

They drove farther north.

Helen had never mentioned having children before, but he felt the weight of it now. "When you got hurt, I thought you were going to die and I'd be left with nothing," she finally said, and he knew she was mourning the family they would never have. Now all they had for sure was each other. Her body must have told her that, and when he'd been shocked and almost killed, she was as close to left alone as she'd ever been. All they really had was a trust that they'd be there for each other, and she had draped that trust over herself like a plaster cast until it was the only thing holding her up.

When they got back to the cabin it was past dark. There was cloud cover pocked with clusters of dense, bright stars.

Helen stepped inside the cabin, took off her boots, and made a show of tossing them far across the room. She undid her belt and slipped her pants to her knees before even taking off her coat. He watched as she kicked her legs free of her jeans, then started undoing the jacket as she walked toward the bedroom, looking over her shoulder at him before the jacket hit the wood floor.

They had not had sex since his accident, and everything she did now made him anxious, but he followed her into the room.

Inside the doorframe she moved behind Terrance and jumped on him. He felt her bare breast push into his back. He turned her over in front of him and pinned her back against the wall. He bent down and took her breast into his mouth and bit down on her nipple with his lips folded over his teeth. She pushed him away and threw herself on the bed. When he came near her, she reached up and scratched his chest. He jumped back and felt the pain of each long nail gouge she'd given him. Her eyes were locked on him. She was gyrating her hips at him, grinding the space between them away, as if, since this part of their lives together was going to be fruitless, she'd make it into something else entirely.

He charged her. When she tried to scratch him again, he blocked her hands and pinned her to the bed and started fucking her immediately. It felt like the first time there was real hate between them, as they crashed their bodies into each other until they'd shook the painting of Priscilla the Performer on the wall sideways.

"Where did that come from?" Terrance asked after they had finished, breaking the silent shock they were both panting into.

"Sometimes I want to be able to yell it out of me," she said.

"This is a good place to do that," he whispered to her as she burrowed her head into the nook of his shoulder and arm.

Helen slept like their sex had erased time and she'd forgotten everything they'd said. Their fight kept Terrance on edge, so he slept poorly and woke before dawn. He got dressed and went out to walk the woods.

Terrance went to see what he had caught in the critter cages he'd set up—his grandfather had taught him to trap, too. When he found a baby raccoon in one of the cages, the animal was swaying back and forth and climbing upside down in a frenzied motion of circles. It was making high-pitched staccato squeaks like an engine stuck in some high gear. Terrance opened the cage to release it, and as it scurried into the trees he hoped he'd never see it again.

Walking back to the cabin, he heard Helen screaming on the porch. From that morning, all through the next month, when Terrance was working with his bones in the woods, he heard her screaming. It became a part of her morning calisthenics. Terrance knew it frightened all the animals in the valley. He tried not to let it bother him. He focused on the bone statue he was building. The creature was eight feet high and had 154 bones, from nine different animals.

He'd started drawing where the bones would go to support the skeleton when he was in the hospital dreaming his own bones back to life. He had since studied charts of the human skeleton. At the taxidermy shop in town, he studied the charts of animal bones. He had learned how museums framed their skeletons, but he wanted his sculpture to be more organic, the way Catrin's steel sculptures always looked like they were stemming from the earth they stood on. He used a papier-mâché system with plaster and strips of old white sheets he bought at a local Salvation Army. He dipped the strips of sheet in a five-gallon bucket of plaster and used the strips to make joints that held the bones. When the plaster dried he wound the joints tighter with thin rope or chicken wire for extra support.

For the bone creature's hands, he used six-point mule deer antlers. The hands connected to the metacarpal bones of a horse, bound by plaster at the elbow joints to a horse femur. The bulbous end of the femur, where the stifle joint had connected, was stuck into the groove of a moose's shoulder plate.

The spine was the hardest part. He let the river clean away the tendons from all the skeletons he had, so the individual vertebrae fell apart from each other. He fed the length of a steel rod through a garden hose and wove the tip of the hose through each open ringlet of spine. For ribs, he connected the humerus and ulna bones of wild turkeys and kept them bent in at the joint like curled fingers. The statue had six ribs on each side, and there was enough room between rib tips for him to kneel between and set the vertebra bones.

Helen did not know what he was doing. It seemed important that she not know. This was his own thing. A project that could keep him straight even while she was slipping. It kept him out in the fresh air, where he felt healthy and alive.

The buffalo skull with the black bear's jaw melded to it was the last thing for him to mount on the sculpture. He had to hook a wire from the top of the skull to each shoulder to keep it on steady. Once it was secure, he brushed off the new snow, stepped back from it and looked up at what he had made.

It looked like a monster emboldened to dance among the trees. He thought about what the muscles of the animal he'd created would look like and how they would curve around the bones as he had them laid out. None of it seemed like something a god would sit down and take the time to figure out. As he walked around it, he wondered what a blue shock would do for the bone marionette he'd created. He considered burying his settlement money right underneath it.

He heard Helen screaming from the deck of the cabin. He sat in the snow at the base of the sculpture and looked at its right foot. He worked his way up, one bone at a time, making sure he had forgotten nothing. He studied the linkage of bones. He shut his eyes and let his mind run over the bones he'd felt in his own body.

Helen screamed again. He let her dirge stretch out and disappear across the valley of his mind. If they were lucky, this place would let them purge his teal-blue current and her deep sadness into the woods. The woods could absorb her wanting children. The woods could absorb the limbo of regret over the kind of father he had been and the broken connections to his own three children.

He wanted to help her. He wondered if his three distant children would ever forgive him for leaving. Maybe they would come out for the summers with whatever kids they might have and give Helen a makeshift family. He would write them this week and tell all three about the settlement money. How he could pay for them to come. How he could send them each a third. They could forgive him. He could forgive himself. They could get horses. There could be dogs. There was life yet. He was constructing a life deep in the forest. It was new life from old life—old bones. That was something he could do for her. He could scramble what they had and lay it at her feet until it made a family and she felt she had something to care for, and sleeping could have mercy on her.

On the way back to the cabin he saw Helen's footprints in the freshly fallen snow. He followed them out of the woods. In the clearing, they had been windswept and disappeared.

He kicked the clumps of snow off his boots by slapping them against the porch banister. Inside the cabin the bedroom door was open. She wasn't in bed. Under the bed in a shoebox were Polaroids of his old life with his children. Some nights when he could not sleep he reached in and took one picture out at random and held it by the corner he had yanked it from the camera and shook it into focus. In the middle of those nights he would try to imagine himself back into the image, imagine pulling those children closer. He wanted to reach into the box now but he listened for bathroom noises. Helen had been taking multiple showers throughout the day lately. She'd once told him she needed a shower to fully wake her up and start her day. Now he was afraid she didn't like what was happening and kept trying to start again.

When he didn't hear any water running, he walked to the bathroom, but the door was open. Fingernail clippings clung to the bottom of the wastebasket by the door. Half a dozen opaque crescents.

At the front door her parka was still on the hook, and her boots, though wet, were still on the floor.

"Helen," he called out in the cabin. No one answered. He opened the front door and stepped onto the porch. The wide clearing extended in front of him to the forest sloping up the mountainside. The lone road cut a line through the center of the field where he'd plowed with his truck. "Helen."

At the far end of the snow-covered open space he saw a herd of mule deer moving along the wall of pines and larches. He followed their movements until he saw her. She was lying naked on her side with her back to him. He took the porch steps in one bound. The closer he got to where she was, the more the woods seemed to recede before becoming a solid wall of conifer trunks.

A blank cloud of terror drained the color out of everything as he ran. As he got closer he saw how the light pooled between her shoulder blades. The deer were trying to move faster through the snow. For a moment he thought about running right past her and into the deeper woods, where he would be clear of her. Then he noticed the deep blue veins on her mid-thigh. They were dead-thing-colored, and that color blue filled his head, blanketing everything like the sky. His last steps were through snow up to his hips, and he lunged forward, crawling to her like a wolverine. The weight of his body pushed snow against her bare back, and he pulled her into his lap and arms, so she was facing him. Her hair was covered in frost. Her body shivered violently. The dark patch of her pubic hair puffed out against the white snow between her legs. She was limp and amoeba-like. He wanted to crack open his ribs and drape himself over her like a jacket. The deer were still marching along the line of trees. Their wet, sable eyes fixated on him leaning over her as if he were in some skewed nativity.

"Helen!" he yelled into her face. The sound of her name fanned out. The deer all jumped, and he heard them crashing away. "Helen." Her eyes were open wide like he'd scared her. Her head was cold when he put his hands against her and red where her cheek was resting in the snow. She looked like an alcoholic Eve—and though his first wife's drinking sickened him, here Helen was beautiful if no less tragic. The last of the deer were passing them about fifty feet away.

She watched him. Then she looked beyond him into the woods.

He lifted her, and she felt lighter than he expected, like part of her, the part he knew, had escaped into the deeper parts of the forest and was now gone.

When he brought her inside, the cabin smelled like burned apples; it was warm compared to her skin against his arms. In the foyer, the *creak* and *pop* of the bones of the cabin settling in broke through the uninterrupted sound of her breathing against his shoulder.

He put her in bed and wrapped the heavy blankets around her. He lay on the covers with his arm and leg over her to keep her warm. Her dark outline made him feel as if she were scratching out from under a thick layer of ice.

"What were you doing in the snow?" he asked. "What were you thinking?" He no longer knew what to do with her, and it frightened him. He held her until he felt her body warming up. He wished he could tune in to what she was thinking like a radio and listen without her knowing, so he could understand what she needed from him.

He went to the bathroom and started the bathtub running with warm water. There was a film of soap in the curve at the base that ringed the whole basin. He had not cleaned the cabin since his accident. He kept his fingers under the water to make sure it was warm but not hot, the way she liked it.

He went back into the bedroom. He flung the blankets back and led her to the tub. He held her arm as she lifted herself over the tub wall and sat down. She leaned her head back until it was under the water, which was clear, and he looked at her naked body. He knew every part of it—had both longed for and hated it. He knew the cluster of freckles above the knob of her left ankle that disappeared when she had a tan. She dunked her head underwater again. When she popped back up, her eyes were raw, and he knew he couldn't help her.

He hated when she smoked but went to her purse and grabbed her lighter and cigarettes. He sat on the toilet next to the tub and put a cigarette in her mouth and lit it. She held it in her lips, and he watched the tip breathe red. Her knee was sticking out of the water, and he wanted to put his hand on it but didn't. Her silence seemed like she was falling into some chasm he could not comprehend. He took the cigarette from her lips and put it back to her mouth when she wanted another drag.

He had sat on that toilet with her leaning over him the time he lanced a cyst on his scalp. It had been there his whole life that he could remember, but in bed she kept running her hand over it and saying it was getting bigger. "I'm taking you to the doctor," she'd say. "It's a tumor!"

She'd done that enough that he found himself running his fingers through his hair to find it, pushing the bump that felt like a hard pea under the skin. He held the tip of the needle under the flame from his Zippo lighter and jammed it into the bump until it scraped his skull. When he pulled out the needle and started to pinch the cyst, she sopped up what came out with a paper towel.

"That's gross," she said. "It's like black pus."

He squeezed and ran his thumb over the area where the bump had been until it felt like a tiny, deflated balloon. She held the paper towel in front of him and smiled because he had wanted to see what was inside. The darkened paper smelled pungent and human.

He passed the cigarette back to her. She had used his

toothbrushes, picked up their used condoms off the floor, stuck her finger in his ear, tickled his armpit, cried on his shoulder that she'd also hit and bit and screamed into. He remembered all those things; time was stacking them, and each left some impression on him because unlike his first wife, his children, those drinking days, he never forgot anything with Helen. Now the memory of her bluing skin somehow became linked to all his other bad memories, and he wondered if that was what her episodes were like, and if each was a new tributary, some minor river pulling them apart.

As he sat on the toilet breathing in her smoke and steam, he felt truly powerless to help her, to find something he could do for her. He sat there breathing in the smoke, her naked body, and the memory of his own black blood.

"So, what are we going to name it?" Helen asked, and pointed to the corner of the bathroom, toward the woods Terrance had been working in. Her voice made it sound like he had done it all for her.

He looked down at her and thought maybe it was defeat that really brought people together. He stepped into the tub and sat behind her. He let the warm water fill the space between his clothes and skin and sagged down so she could lean against him and he could hold her up.

9

John Parks, 2000

I had packed the Land Rover and Thule roof rack for an escape, a full break from the world, and while doing it, had imagined going without her. There were full blue water jugs and red plastic gasoline cans, a tent, mosquito net, folding chairs, tarps, rope, a rusty machete I'd gotten at the flea market, sleeping bags, books, maps, water filters, tools, mess kits, pots, a Coleman propane camp stove, and a lamp with a box of extra propane tanks. I had a telescope, rain and beach gear, dried and canned fruit, an ax, fishing poles, guidebooks for identifying fish, waders for surf fishing, and tackle boxes I'd slowly assembled, adding lures and weights from every gear shop across the county. There were liquor bottles and two ice chests. There was an air compressor to let air out of the tires so they would grip better in the soft sand, and then fill them up again for harder surfaces. I had winches, cables, binoculars—things I'd bought at REI, North Face, L.L.Bean, and West Marine. There was enough to start my own crisscrossing line around the globe. I was in full-blown daydream mode when Jamie came out into the garage and tossed a box of her favorite candy in the back, Mamba fruit chews, which she ordered by the case online.

We crossed the border in San Luis, Arizona, and during our first several days of driving we passed soon-to-be ghost towns with their turquoise-, red-, and green-painted taquerias filling the air with the scent of fresh tortillas. We stopped at a roadside restaurant, sat on Naugahyde seats, and ate flank steak covered in hot mole sauce that we squeezed fresh limes over for break-fast. We bought Cokes from a faded red vending machine, and when we finished those, Jamie wanted an orange soda from the illuminated cooler behind the counter. She was thirsty from our dusty drive, during which we kept breathing in the fine dirt in the air until it crusted at the corners of our mouths. The woman behind the counter poured the soda into a plastic bag, put a straw in, and twisted the bag around the straw so she could keep the bottle for the deposit. Jamie drank from the sack of orange fluid like it was some kind of neon IV bag.

After eating, Jamie drove and I watched each weedy road disappear into the shimmer of the surrounding desert. We drove in silence, passing acres of poor, red soil webbed with cracks and deep ridges full of long scratchy blades of grass that swayed, bent, and cast shadows, but were worthless to everything but stray horses. At the edge of the small towns on the map, we passed shacks made of scrap metal and rotting lumber with corrugated sheets of tin and frayed brown tarps for walls tucked away in the trees. Feral hounds dug in the ditches. Men with tooled leather cheeks and thick black mustaches scissor-trimmed into neat lit-tle tents for their upper lips, and old women with faces as etched and furrowed as the landscape drank something steaming hot out of aluminum cans in the blue morning light.

I'd been careless with the water at the start of our trip and it gave me rotgut. When Jamie pulled over I dug little holes in the sand with the heel of my boot, squatted over them and left splatters of my own excrement along the road like sloppy cairns marking our way home. It was while squatting over one of those pits that I caught my wife staring at me from the driver's seat. Her sharp gaze was leveled on my hands pinching at the double roll of flesh at my abdomen and the eggplant purple scarring running up my side.

"What are you doing?" she asked.

"Nothing."

I really looked at her then, and maybe it was the golden cast of the light narrowing her eyes, or maybe she was concerned by my frequent stops, but it felt like she was in some way disappointed in me.

We kept driving south along asphalt and dirt paths, then no roads whatsoever, stopping only when I felt sick again. I'd run off into the dark scrub brush that Jamie said looked like giant wooden spiders crawling over the dunes. In the hard, sunbaked sand everything was quiet, foreboding. When I was done I shut my eyes to feel the sun on my face and let the ticking of the radiator lead me back to Jamie.

In the town of Guaymas, a group of boys were playing in the surf with a giant piece of Styrofoam that must have been used to pack an industrial refrigeration unit or something. One of the boys was wearing a blue mesh basketball jersey with cracked white numbers on the back, a dull two and eight faded at the sides. All the other boys were naked as they swam around the floating Styrofoam, clinging to it and riding it back to the shore where little dollops of it broke off. Their skin, wet and glossy as river mud, glinted as they danced wildly on top of their pontoon before crashing into the water. Jamie took pictures of them, then folded her arms under her breasts and watched.

"They're having fun," she said.

"What are they saying?"

"They're just roughhousing," she said as their voices washed ashore.

We left Guaymas and drove farther south to Zihuatanejo, where we picked up enough food and water supplies to last a month, and kept driving south until we hit a long stretch of open, undeveloped coast that had wide beaches and sand dunes off the bluff. I let air out of the tires and we drove along the high-water mark until we found a good place to set up camp on a wide mound off the beach. There was plenty of driftwood for fires scattered like creeping mantises along the sand knolls. I set the tent up as Jamie explored the area. When I finished I found her standing on a rock in a tide pool. The base of the rock had barnacles around it that latched on at high tide. Her silhouette reflected off the surface. I looked closely at both visions of her then, as if I could see her inner life running its secret course.

"Why are you looking at me like that?" she asked.

"Just looking," I said, hesitant to start a conversation after we had avoided them for so long. Though what I wanted to say, more than anything was, *My God, you're a gorgeous woman. How do I keep you?*

The rest of that day we gathered all the driftwood we could find into an enormous pile. It was the first task we'd done together. When we each grabbed an end of log and hauled it across the sand, it was clear we'd gathered enough for many nights of campfires. When we laid the log down on the pile, the gesture felt like a silent agreement that this was a spot where we both wanted to stay for a long time, as there was nothing there—nothing to remind us of where we had come from.

For almost half of a year, we had kept 3-D ultrasound pictures of a baby that looked like a doughy octopus hidden in some shadowy underwater cave stuck to our refrigerator under a Home Depot magnet. The head was mashed in fleshy folds, and we took the pictures down each night and looked at them, talking each other through the magical asymmetry of the heart pulling to the left, the liver developing on the right and the lungs taking on their distinct shapes. The genetic counselor told us afterward those pictures never hinted at a problem. She used a flip chart and pencil drawings of chromosomes to explain what went wrong, named the problem *omphalocele*, but none of that ever added up when accounting for the crushing fatigue that set in when I saw my daughter born. A dark snake started writhing inside of me, and the soft nudges of anxiety I'd been feeling during Jamie's pregnancy exploded into crushing disbelief. She came out blue and silent. There was a fist-size opening in the middle of her abdominal wall and a thin layer of slick bloody membrane at the base of her umbilical cord was the only thing that held back her protruding intestines. She gave a quick cry from the corner of the room and began to turn red under the lights. That was the only time I saw her before the doctor swept her away to the operating room. That was the only time I ever saw her.

After we came home from the hospital we turned some awful corner of our life. Because we'd already weathered the years of my deployments, injury, and the long passage back into each other's inner lives, I felt like the future, just as it was laying itself out in front of me like a wide, flat sky, was snake-bit and soured.

The ultrasound pictures stayed under the magnet for over a month after my daughter was born until one day they were gone. I don't know what Jamie did with them, if she put them in a box where she kept scraps of her secret life or if she got rid of them completely, but those pictures had somehow been keeping me together. Without them I was left with a need to know what happened. I understood what the genetic counselor showed us but I wanted to know more than that. I wanted to add things up, to know what forces led things to go so wrong.

I watched Jamie through the smoke of our driftwood fire our first night on that Mexican beach. The ocean breeze kept the flies away but at night moths fluttered blindly around our campfire, dodging the floating embers. We cooked sausages and drank warm beers by the fire and then walked after the sunset along the strand. When our feet cut through the soft surf and the breeze brought the sweet smell of seaweed and smoke, it was easy to fantasize about living there forever.

Night after night I took out my telescope and spun it around the sky as the moon was bitten down to a small thumbnail and then was blotted out.

When she was young, Jamie's father had left their family in

an attempt to save himself and his kids from his alcoholism and went back west. After that, the West became a mythical place to reinvent yourself for her. That was why she had come, though now, we were realizing the sky and land were so vast that to make a place for yourself was no small thing.

During the day we walked for hours on the shore, amazed by what washed up: trees, shells, large strips of fishing nets, life jackets, glinting pieces of sea glass that sprawled about as if the sand had eyes.

I grabbed a drink from the ice chest and went to piss behind a scrub bush. There was a little lizard sunning itself on a rock. Along the shore a sandpiper was running up and down with the surf, dancing in that in-between place of land and water. Out at sea, pelagic birds bobbed on the surface, dipping their heads under to snatch at some plankton bloom. Jamie was coming out of the water and she was shining—her shoulders and long limbs tan. I craved to know every endless illumination of her body as I once had. I wanted to know how she felt about me. We were faced with a choice: to want each other or to be away from each other. The question hung over us and our movements.

I had bought licenses and saltwater fishing stamps. Read about fishing from the coast and how to wade out into the surf. The book explained how to use weights and bobbers to fish for midrange and bottom feeders, redfish, and sea bass. Jamie made a pitcher of tequila drinks, squeezed in a fresh lime and dropped in spoonfuls of salt to cut the sharp taste. When we had drunk enough and were starting to feel a heavy buzz, we built up a giant driftwood fire that we left burning on the beach until the haze from the fire rose in a column and mushroomed out overhead.

There was a high wind coming off the water when we walked into the shallows, knee-deep the first fifty yards, gradually dipping up to our hips about fifty yards past that. Clouds were hurrying past the moon. Spray misted our faces. When we were deep enough, we spread out from each other and hurled our hooks baited with freezer-dried shrimp into the dark waters where we couldn't see them land. Jamie swayed each time a small wave passed through her, and the bait bag she'd draped over her shoulder rose up on its side and sat on the water. Sparkling orange firelight lit the water's surface behind us. I slowly spun the reel, culling the lure back before tossing it back out to be lost in the enormity of the ocean around us.

On my sixth or seventh cast, something big struck at my line and the tip of my rod curved violently downward until my fists were both underwater. I let the line run out and listened to the wheezing of the reel.

I yelled to Jamie, who was ten yards from me, hip-deep in the ocean like she was the only person on earth.

Whatever it was, it was stronger than I was expecting. I yanked the rod to set the hook, put the lock on the reel, and started backpedaling. I fought the fish, arching the rod upward until it bent so much I was afraid it would break, then cranked in the reel as I leaned the rod down. We were a long way from our fire. Our sleeping bags airing out in the sand looked like wilted slug-skins. The line stretched over my head and disappeared into the water somewhere out of sight. The image of an old *Far Side* cartoon of a submarine streaming along with a fishing pole dragging behind it popped into my head, and I almost laughed, but then the line darted toward Jamie.

"It's coming toward you," I yelled. "Shine the flashlight out there."

She let her beam of light search out the spot where my line submerged and found it a few feet in front of her. I kept reeling, fighting, until I saw a triangular dorsal fin cut the surface and slide across a swell.

I felt it in my bones that the future wasn't promised to us.

"Jesus," Jamie gasped, and started running toward me. Freezer-dried shrimp floated loose from her bag and fanned out in her wake.

Please, please, please. I took desperate, heart-pounding strides toward her, both running and swimming, fueled by that old feeling of loving her more than myself. *Please don't sink beneath the waves.*

It was a hammerhead shark, probably five feet long, with that gray board planked onto its head, holding those dark globe eyes out to the side. When Jamie was next to me the dorsal fin swayed closer to us and began to thrash at the water's surface. I pulled my fillet knife from my side and cut the line loose. I staggered backward and Jamie caught me. Her arms wrapped around my ribs and met in a fist at my heart.

The shark slipped off and disappeared.

I cut her bait bag loose and tossed it away.

"Can we be done doing this now?" she asked.

"Yes," I said, and we held each other's hands as we worked our way back to the shallows. What else might have been swimming around our legs?

On shore, we stuck the ends of our rods into the sand and passed another pitcher of her tequila drink between us. I let the salted liquor slide down my throat and spread out in my stomach and felt that warmth settle there. Jamie took off her bikini bottoms, wrung them out, and draped them over the back of the camp chair. She put on her baggy blue cargo shorts and a faded yellow tank top with spaghetti straps that pressed tight over her shoulders.

In the dark by the firelight, having navigated a knife-edge, our fear slowly began to slip away like a whisper and something finally gave way between us.

"I'm not sure what we're supposed to be doing," she said. She was looking down at her feet. Her voice was soft and I knew it was time we showed each other our own sad truths.

"I am trying," I said.

"Trying what, John?"

"To see what will happen to us." I took courage and kept talking, letting what might have been gibberish spiral out of me. "I think we're both terrified to try to have another child together." *Shut up. Shut up*, blared out in my head, but I kept going until it felt like some detached voice was speaking for me. "I've been too afraid to tell you how I felt because I didn't want to guilt you into staying with me. I wanted to give you an out because you can still remarry and have your own children." My voice was low. "But the thought of it kills me," came out as soft as rabbit's breath.

She didn't say anything for a long time. Her hands worked at the hem of her cargo shorts. Then her lips started moving, teasing out empty words until she found her voice. "When we came home without her, I hated you for pretending some ordinary peace had settled over us."

"You don't love me anymore," I said.

Her eyes shot up and narrowed on me. She was looking at me then. Full-on looking at me—taking everything about me in, and I felt her disdain for me puncture deep, far deeper than the exploding side of the navy ship did or the hammerhead's teeth could have reached.

I waited for her to say something else, but she pressed her palms into her eyes and sat there. The fire popped and hissed as it ate into the dry driftwood. I wanted us to keep talking, getting everything out in the open. But she said nothing and eventually stood up and went into the tent.

I sat alone under the stars for what felt like hours until the wind picked up off the water and a storm started flashing in the distance. I crawled into the tent beside her and lay there without saying anything. I felt husked, like something essential had been pared back and bared my raw heart.

During the delivery at the hospital, we were each other's caretakers. I wanted time to curve back on itself and find us like we were then, before we knew what was going to happen, before we went home where the absence of her large stomach did not match the quiet of the house.

Later that night an ocean storm blew in, churning the frothy waves up and smashing them on the beach. I unzipped the corner of the tent's mesh window and pushed my face into the netting to feel the spray from the swirl of rain and see the ocean light up in the distance and listen to the storm crawl over us on lightning legs, its belly dragging like a heavy sheet.

"Let's go out," Jamie whispered.

I didn't know she was awake.

"Let's go out there. Let's go now," she said.

We went out and ran in the rain. It was warm. Our feet slapped against the wet sand. The rain drummed off my shoulders and rolled in big wet beads off my scalp and down the back of my ears. When we ran out of breath far down the strand, I hunched over with my hands braced on my knees. My ribs hurt. Jamie stood beside me, and though it was too dark to really see her face, I knew she was looking at me. Then she reached out and took a wild swing at my face.

"Don't say that," she said as her fist landed on the meaty center of my upper lip. Then she tried to leg-sweep me. "Don't say I don't love you." I braced myself, pushed her to the ground, and when I climbed on top of her, she started pulling at my swim trunks and when they were down we started grinding each other into the sand. We let the waves ride up and pull us out until we were floating. We sloshed each other around in the water in a breathless struggle. Then we slammed back into the sand.

I laid there on the beach afterward, looking through the rain for stars in the dark sky. I'd heard how in the seventies NASA sent out sounds of the human body into space, the *da Dum da Dum da Dum* of a heartbeat; breathing, both steady and wild; greetings in fifty-five languages; and music by Beethoven, Blind Willie Johnson, and Chuck Berry. I thought of those thrumming sounds, pulses of interstellar vocals traveling so far. Jamie and I had let our hurt sit for too long. There were impossible distances between us neither of us knew how to address. We had only our suffering, our desire to send out to each other. Such meager wailing probes.

The night passed in a flash. I shut my eyes on the wet beach and then opened them and the night was over. The sun was already coming up. I woke alone and walked away from our tent for about a mile. There was a large hollowed-out fish on the beach that shimmered with iridescent blue flies bubbling out of a gash in its side. The steady buzzing sounded angry, hungry. Farther down the beach there were four men at the edge of the trees, shirtless, barefoot; each held a machete that dangled like menacing fangs glinting in the sun. They were facing my direction and I stopped before going any farther. There was no fat on any of them. Each had chestnut skin and glossy black hair. Their features seemed to blend together in the distance. They watched me for so long I imagined them running toward me, all swinging arms and steel blades, that these were the kind of people you read about in newspapers, chopping tourists up and scattering their limbs around the dunes. I imagined running toward them too, my arms wide-open, embracing that fate. Then one of the men turned inland and grabbed a large mesh bag of coconuts I hadn't seen and the others followed, leaving me alone again with my wife on that empty coastline.

That afternoon we explored the dunes and swam in the ocean when the waves came in. We didn't talk much for fear of stopping whatever dormant want had woken between us. That night we both drank too much and passed out in our tent. It was a bad night. I kept slipping in and out of half sleep and dreams about a black stone fist pummeling Jamie's abdomen. When I woke I put on a pair of jeans that were bunched at the foot of the tent and grabbed a flashlight. Outside I shone the pitiful light beam on the dead embers of our fire and scooped a handful of ashes into my fist and brought it to my nose—the scent of something dead lingered. I took off my clothes, walked into the surf, and lay down so the water covered the bottom half of my body. I floated in the subtidal sands and let them pack me into the beach. The water seemed so immense that the ocean could only be expanding away from me. The residue of that strange old life was being scrubbed off my body. In the surf, it was like I was clear of the world.

I climbed back into our tent, water dripping on the thin nylon floor. I leaned over Jamie and pressed myself down on her, a salty flesh puddle. I peeled her from her L.L.Bean sleeping bag, and loose-fit yoga pants, and fingered the elastic of her cotton underwear so I could pull them down. I sunk my face into her soft, sweet neckline. The hot skin of her thighs clamped onto my hips so hard I knew I'd feel them long after we finished.

Afterward, lying at the foot of the tent I bent down and bit the toenail on her big toe so it snapped between my teeth and left a nasty white barb flailing off the end of her foot.

"Gross," she said, and pulled her knees up to her chest where she hugged them close. I was paralyzed then by some voltage of light that flashed in her cool green eyes, her wet red mouth, and the momentary softening of her features that offered a glimpse at the unburdened woman I had married. I shut my eyes and kept that image of her in my head—stacked upon the layers of other moments with her.

I woke in the morning and everything was new and frigid, and when I realized Jamie wasn't next to me I felt my heart giving. Above her side of the tent I could see where she'd traced little interconnected symbols overhead in the condensation.

I sat in front of the tent until she walked back down the beach toward me. She was topless. She had suntan lines from wearing her bikini. I was arrested by the sight of her as I shamelessly studied her body. I knew that body so well. I had seen every minute of her pregnancy and held her close as we rocked back and forth, contractions racking her stomach and back, pain-induced moans billowing from her chest like the calls of a giant dying bird. I had seen how her chest caved in when the nurse came back into our room, her eyes revealing everything, after the doctors had done their best to save our daughter. How much more intimate could two people get?

Late that afternoon she poured us each a glass of her tequila drink. Condensation on her glass beaded up and streamed down like tears before she palmed it, drank, and then touched the glass to her cheek to feel the coolness. We finished that pitcher and made another as it got dark.

The beautiful beach and isolation on the unencumbered surf rolling up the sand had been enchanting enough to believe the escape fantasy we told ourselves. Jamie grabbed a pack of Mamba and put a few in her mouth. She sucked them into one ball she rolled around with her tongue until her breath smelled like raspberry. As I was sitting in the lawn chair she bent down and kissed me and pushed the chewed wad into my mouth directly from the pocket of her cheek. Quiet, secret messages passed between us. I prayed the most compressed prayer.

When we needed to resupply, we packed up our camp and drove back north to Zihuatanejo. We rented a room in the old part of town, away from the tourists, in a two-story hotel with high arched windows that looked down onto the honey-colored cobblestone street full of rusted cars below. The scent of wet trash and cooked meat rose up on the breeze that brushed back our curtains. Quick voices I couldn't understand and a steady churning of vague noise drifted past, but at the windowsill with my wife it didn't feel strange being there. This was as fine a place as any to face life. A hard knot began to unravel in my chest and I felt something was over and something else had begun.

We showered together, slowly washing the salt out of each other's hair with vanilla-scented shampoo. Then we walked to the zocalo, and through the town square to the water. When she hooked her arm around mine as we walked I felt like crying.

In town, Jamie asked a passing woman to take our picture. She handed the camera over and the woman held it up to her face and adjusted it to frame the two of us in the backdrop of the sunset on the fish market. The direct sunlight was bringing out the full color of the woman's clothing, as if this stranger in front of us was suddenly glowing. All of this had been necessary, all of it, just for this photo to keep us bound together—to mark the good moments that can liberate us from misery and offer hope. Hope we could come through even this, through anything. That whole trip had been an ongoing act of surrender—mercurial, but helping me flow back to my wife. The camera flashed, and Jamie said something with rolling *r*'s and she squeezed her arms against my hip so I knew she had asked the woman to take another photo, just to be sure.

10

Connor Thurber, 2005

I don't know what to do about my son. His friends have nick-named him "Gonzo," and I fear this has added pressure or given him license to act crazy. He's just limped home with torn clothes and a three-inch gash in his thigh he got from his friend Adler running full speed behind a shopping cart with my son hunkered inside. Adler let go before the rattling cart's wheels slammed into the raised parking lot curb and launched Dennis through the air, where he landed as planned in the ungroomed pine bush. I'm sure Dennis thought he was some kind of hero as he heard his friends gather around the bush that swallowed him, laughing, "Gonzo. Gonzo, are you all right?"

I sit him on the toilet seat lid in my condo to clean the cut that will add to his growing collection of scars. I pat an aloe-soaked cloth on his left leg where it looks like someone has scraped a potato peeler over the skin. On the counter is a plaster cast of a deer's hoofprint we made together when he was nine years old. Based on his bony shoulders, even if he has a late growth spurt like I did, he'll probably still be scrawny and lean when he comes out of his teens. He's fourteen now, my only child. He spends Thursday through Sunday morning with me and the rest of the week with my ex-wife, Dyla, and her new husband, Tom. He waits until he's with me to try his stunts.

Dyla made me pay to send him to a psychologist to see what "his cries for help" were all about.

"Nothing, I thought it would be cool" was what he told me when I asked him what really made him do these things.

"He's a teenage boy," was what Dr. Mujardi told me after I paid him 120 bucks for talking to Dennis for an hour. I want to believe Dr. Mujardi. That he's a teenager and hasn't evened the scales of broken bones and good judgment yet.

"He's not doing this stuff at my house," Dyla told me. "He's seeking attention from you, or showing resentment toward you."

She still knew how to hurt me.

Dennis was eight when our problems started boiling over and consuming our home life. It's hard for me to think of what sort of damage I'm responsible for in my son's psyche that makes him want to jump off houses onto trampolines that launch him into pools. When he tried that stunt he overshot the water and broke his forearm on the pool's concrete lip. His friends had to drag him out of the water, where he was floating on his back, his good arm holding the broken one to his chest, while he screamed the best he could between spitting up chlorine water. When he was twelve, he biked off the top bleacher of the high school football stadium, as if he thought he'd land gracefully or fly, and sprained his knee and broke his left thumb. I can't even guess at all the other things he's done that I've never found out about because he wasn't hurt bad enough for me to know.

Dyla asked me to leave soon after he turned ten. I had to work more and travel more to pay for both a place of my own and alimony payments. I can't help but feel that soon after that, with my absence, something weight-bearing in him shifted. The thought makes me forget the pain of my marriage falling apart; all that gets eclipsed in the suffocating feeling that I wasn't there for him. I'd become the kind of father I resented my own dad for being. It makes me think of his whole life so far as a series of miniature sections, of how he needed me in different ways and of how at every division I must have let him down.

When my marriage ended, it gave me a haunting sense of vertigo and an overwhelming desire to still be loved by my ex-wife. I spent my work nights on the road, either walking around whatever town I was in, or writhing in the dark, pining away for a woman, or anything that could help distract me from the fear that I would spend the rest of my life alone. I eventually started going online to meet new women, but each attempt felt so weighted by my own desperation to fill this void in my life, I was always left disappointed.

Then Dyla met Tom. Tom owned a contracting company and designed his own house. It's gigantic. Dyla and Dennis moved in soon after it was completed. I had been traveling to the mid-Atlantic states during the week to sell ball bearings for a manufacturer out of the north suburbs of Buffalo. I worked for them right out of school for a spell, and they rehired me because I told them what I think any wise employer would want to hear: that I was young, which meant I had energy, and that I had a wife and a young kid, which meant the frivolousness of my single life no longer existed and I would be diligent in the tasks they gave me, because I had to be. It was the great shift of my life, from the world holding possibilities to it holding responsibilities. When the divorce was final, I worked even harder to keep myself busy, and with the efforts came more clients, more sales reps, and more time I needed to spend in my territory. Now I spend my days calling on large, bombed-out foundries and assembly plants, and eating dinners alone before trying to sleep in hotel rooms that all seem sad in the same lonely way. I travel Sunday night through Wednesday night. The rest of the week I'm around for Dennis, but it's during my absence that he must soak up his need to fly, or retaliate against me in some way.

A coworker invites me to watch a football game with him at a local bar. I used to love football, but now I don't care for it, so I pass. I think of a friend telling me years ago about going to a Buffalo Bills game and seeing a stadium filled with fans standing up and cheering, all leaning forward, like the place was going to swallow itself. All that money, time, and energy.

Instead, I sit alone and watch one of the shows Dennis likes, *Jackass*, in my hotel room in a La Quinta inn across from the Newark airport. It scares me that my son is emulating these quickly aging young drunks. The stars of the show stick toy cars up their asses and get X-rays to shock the emergency room doctors, and put their sock-clad penises into a snake cage until they're bitten. It makes me uncomfortable because some of these daring acts remind me of my own unsupervised childhood and the self-inflicted violence of playing with my neighborhood friends. I look out the window, toward the airport. This part of

New Jersey is all highways weaving in and out of New York City. There's a large Anheuser-Busch brewery with a giant, red neon eagle floating above the bold red letters that spell *BUDWEISER*. It looks like a strange god looming over the area, red and royal against all the white lights and blackness.

When my flight lands at Buffalo Niagara late Wednesday night, I walk along the side of the parking garage to get to my car. There is an industrial exhaust pipe blowing warm air on the side of structure. The exhaust is thick white, and I watch a group of flight attendants walk into the cloud and disappear. Random arms and heads emerge like they are fighting their way out, while being pulled deeper into the mist.

When I get to my car I drive straight to Tom's house in the new development of huge houses near Chautauqua Art Institute. I want to see Dennis with his mother and what their time together looks like. It's past eleven when I park up the street from their house. Their place is two stories tall with an attached garage that juts out toward the street. Above the garage is a large strip of windows that looks into the living room. It may have been the driving all over New Jersey for a week—the time alone—or the feeling of dread I got from that red Budweiser sign sticking out among everything else, I don't know, but something makes me creep to the side of their house. I wheel the fifty-gallon plastic garbage bin against the garage wall, climb onto it, and balance my feet at the edges so my weight won't buckle the lid. I reach up so my fingers grasp the edge of the asphalt roof shingles, then I grip the garage siding with the tread of my shoes and kick so I can pull myself high enough to fold my stomach over the garage roof and sneak up. I stay low so that the grainy texture of the shingles feels like hard sandpaper against my forearms as I army-crawl toward the large windows, where I peek into their living room, trying to find the fissure that snapped through my old life.

Dennis is sitting on the couch watching television with Dyla. His feet are stretched out in front of him, and his shoulders slump off the back of the couch so his bird's chest curves inward. Dyla has her feet tucked under her legs and looks like she's about to fall asleep. She slowly runs her hand through her hair so it falls forward over her face. Then she rhythmically sweeps it off to the side and then back over her face again. I can see both youth and age on her face as she reveals it over and over. God, I want to touch her face at that moment. I want to stay here all night and watch them. I realize that this is exactly what I hope will be waiting for me when I am on the road.

A flashlight's beam shines up from the driveway. "What the hell are you doing?" I hear Tom say.

There are no stars above me, just the black night—a slight glow stretching from the halation of the city. After a long pause, I look down at Tom and say, "It's me; it's Connor."

I crawl back across the garage. I lean my chest against the roof so my body is parallel to the edge and let my feet roll off the side, slowly letting my body hang down. My fingers scrape raw from the shingles. Tom holds the flashlight on me as I hang there, afraid to let go, unsure how far down I'll fall. When I do let go, the shock of landing just a few feet below compresses into my knees and I fall back onto the blacktop. On the ground I feel foolish, like I've lost my last strand of grace. I feel a tic under my eyes, like they are trying to shut but can't.

"I wanted to see how he was," I tell Tom, who puts the flashlight down once he's convinced it's really me.

"Maybe you could call or knock on the door," Tom says. "Is this something you do? I mean, do I need to draw the curtains at night?"

"No. I guess I was a bit lonely tonight, and wanted to see him."

Tom looks at me for a moment. "I can understand that," he says, then he stands there as if he's drawn a line that I can't cross, which of course he has to do. But he doesn't push me, as if he's made the decision not to belittle me even since he's found me reduced to this. I drive home that night wondering if he'll tell Dyla or Dennis about me, that above their heads the past tried to break in.

My hands shake as I drive away from Tom's house, and I pull my car over and get out on the southern side of Harmony Road where there are long and wide cornfields lit by the highway. Thousands of Canadian geese that I have been seeing flying overhead for the last month have congregated here. Each has that white chinstrap around their sable-black necks, the identical heave of gray-brown feathered chest, and wet, obsidian eyes. I walk toward the edge of the field where the geese are spread out like a field of dark, bulbous fruit, like rotting watermelons.

At the edge of their mass I make a deep guttural sound and sustain it in a sort of panicked roar as I charge. The first dozen or so birds I approach twitch and do that fly-running thing to get away. I run farther, moving in manic spirals through the flocks. I stride over astonished geese until all I see is the disorder of rising birds. My growling echoes back with the thumping of hundreds of wings and a chorus of irritated honking. A few birds snap at my legs like snakes. I don't stop running. I'm probably trespassing. I'm certainly causing duress to these animals, but I don't stop. The dark bodies haul up from the ground and the sound of their leaping in the part of the field I sprint through sends the rest of them to flight. It's as if the night lifts off the earth instead of falls upon it. I stop yelling and just run and listen. I feel the hammering of my heart, the sweat coating my skin underneath my clothes, and the thumping of all these animals lifting into the sky.

I get almost all of them into the air and stop because I'm exhausted. The swirl of geese over my head is all consuming and small waves of slowly forming V's start peeling off the swarm and fly away. I watch as the geese work their way back into some order. Then I walk back to my car, where in the distance I can see several other cars on the side of the road watching me. I can now hear the cornstalks crunch under my feet, but I can't trace my footprints as the whole field looks churned over from my running and the abrupt departure of all those aerating wings. I know with the departing of the geese comes the freezing winds and heavier snow. I realize there is no hiding from winter. But I also know that somewhere in the middle months of the cold season, I'll need some hope that it will thaw.

The next day I pick Dennis up from school at St. Francis High. Dyla told me to do this on days he stays with me so he wouldn't get so banged up with his friends.

"Bye, Gonzo," I hear one of the boys call to him as he gets into my car.

"Gonzo, huh," I say to Dennis as he settles in next to me. He shifts his hips so he can untuck his white polo shirt from his dark blue slacks. As I drive out of the parking lot, I have to stop for a sports team jogging past in gray sweatpants and maroon sweat-shirts with the head of a wolf stenographed on their backs.

"Which team is this?" I ask Dennis.

"Soccer."

"Would you be interested in joining them?"

"No, Dad," he says, popping hockey puck–size earphones over his ears.

"Well, why not? I know it's not because you're afraid of get-ting hurt. I think it would be good for you."

"I'll pass," he says, then starts drumming his hands on his legs.

"Well, how about joining a band, taking music lessons or something?"

He drums the whole drive home. But this is on par with our interactions, as I'm never sure what to do with him. There were whole days I remember spending with my own father, enjoying the warmth of his attention. My father adjusting the rabbit-ears TV antenna to get the Bills game on. Kool-Aid and Chef Boy-ardee lunches. Hot dogs for dinner. The buns pulled open with our thumbs. Ketchup and root beer smears on our shirts. Not necessarily talking and laughing, but at least being together. It's those small moments I remember and want to build with Dennis.

After a dinner, where the closest thing to communicating with me Dennis did was pouring salt onto the table and making cir-cle designs with his fingertips, I go online to St. Francis High School's webpage to see what sort of extracurricular activity I can sign "Gonzo" up for. The sports page briefly explains that they are called the Wolves because of the story of St. Francis and the Wolf of Gubbio. A giant wolf was terrorizing the people of Gubbio. Each time the people went outside of the gated city, they had to go in well-armed groups, because if a lone traveler met with the wolf, the wolf would devour him. The people asked St. Francis to intervene. Francis went and talked to the wolf, and the wolf told Francis that he was ravenous. So Francis made a deal with the wolf, that if he stopped eating the townspeople, they would feed him, and the wolf agreed. It was the courage to face your problems and the spirit of working together that they were trying to instill in their athletes.

I scroll through the sports teams and see that the cross-country team has started their fall season. Maybe Dennis can run the crazy energy out of himself, I think.

Dennis agrees to sign up for the cross-country team if I buy him the newest PlayStation.

"My little wolf," I say to him when I drop him off at school the next day.

After I drop Dennis off, I go to a local coffee shop where I get a coffee and take a table in the back of the room where I can plug my laptop into a socket.

The sales reps I work with have suggested that I try to set dates up for myself on my trips, so I pull up a Yahoo! Personals site and input the area codes around the Delaware Water Gap, where I'm headed on Sunday night. Lists of bios of women, aged thirty-five to forty-five, fill the screen. I start an online chat with a woman named Meredith, who is a divorced mother of two and works as a purchaser for a fabric design company. She suggests we arrange to talk at the same time the next day.

When I pull into the parking lot of St. Francis later that afternoon, Dennis is waiting for me outside the front of the building.

"How was it?" I ask him as he gets in my car. He's wearing the same clothes he had on in the morning.

"How was what?" he says.

"Your first day of practice."

"I didn't make it today," he says, reaching for his earphones.

"Why not?"

"I got detention, so I couldn't go to practice."

"What did you do?" I ask, feeling a flush of blood hit my face. I'll have to tell Dyla. "You better tell me, Dennis."

"Mr. Tanner got all upset over nothing," he says.

"What. Did. You. Do?"

"I'll show you," he says with a smile on his face. He pulls the fancy new Nokia phone Tom bought him for his last birthday from his backpack.

When I pull the car over to the side of the road, Dennis hits play and aims the little screen at me. It flashes on with someone filming Dennis picking up a cinder block and lying down on the ground with the block on his stomach. Then his friend Adler walks up with a hammer, and after Dennis nods to him, Adler swings the hammer over his head and drops it with all his strength onto the cinder block, which crumbles in pieces on Dennis's body.

"Gonzo, you're nuts," I hear the cameraman say, then the film stops.

"Where was this?" I ask Dennis.

"Behind the gym," he tells me. "Mr. Tanner turned the corner as Adler was hitting the block and it freaked him out because he thought he was trying to kill me or something." He is smiling at me as he says this.

"What is this all about? You've got to stop this shit!" Neither of us says anything until I start the car again. "Where do you get these ideas from?"

"Online," he says.

At home I make him pull up videos on YouTube for me.

"We put some of our stuff up here too," he says with a sort of pride.

"For who?" I ask.

"For everyone. The whole world can see," he says. "Check some of this stuff out." He starts searching for videos and pulls up a clip from an old Indian yogi who lies down on a bed of nails and has an elephant press a massive foot down on his stomach. "You see how strong that guy's stomach is?" His voice betrays a measure of excitement. Then he plays clips of guys BASE jumping off cliffs, shooting friends with Tasers, snowmobiles hitting ramps and flipping completely over in the air, men with shoddy-looking jetpacks shakily rising off the ground; the stunts are endless.

I watch the video clips with Dennis. There are infinite numbers of videos of people being flung around their lives for him to watch. He clicks from one to the next until it becomes clear to me that he has somehow taken this craziness as instruction on how he is supposed to live his own life.

When I drop Dennis off at Tom's that Sunday, Dyla comes out to the car. She stands next to my window and looks inside. I can see a trace of the young woman I met sixteen years earlier. When we met, it took me a criminally long time to realize how beautiful she was.

"Did you hear he got detention?" she asks. "Have you talked with him?"

"Yeah. A bit."

"You have to be tough with him. He doesn't need another friend. He needs you to be his father. Tom can't do everything." At this, I want to swing my car door open so it slams against her kneecap. "He's going to get hurt badly one of these days." She puts her hands on my door and leans in toward me. "Are you doing okay?" she asks.

"I'm fine," I say.

"Well, then, we'll talk more when you pick him up next week." She turns from the car and I start the engine. She says it under her breath, but I hear it as she walks away. "Stay off the roof."

The phrase sinks into my ears and I feel how ridiculous I must seem to her.

Online-Meredith and I meet for a dinner date on Tuesday at a small Mexican restaurant. She told me she was forty-one, but when she walks in she looks older. She has brown hair and hasn't dyed the thin strips of gray that start at her temples and wrap back into her ponytail. She's a large woman, much shorter than me but my weight at least. Her right shoulder slumps a bit forward and down like she's been injured. We talk about our kids, and eat slowly. I tell her about my son floating upside down in the pool with a broken arm. How I have nightmares of the water rising to his chin, flooding his mouth, filling his lungs.

Meredith must have sensed something wanting and vulnerable in me when I tell her this, as later, when we are about to leave, she leans over her drink, polite and without making eye contact, and places her hand on top of mine.

We go to my hotel room at the Fairfield Inn. She follows me in her car. Inside my room she goes to the bathroom and I can hear her peeing through the door. When she comes out she turns the lights off and we get undressed before we even touch each other. As she walks to the bed her breasts hang down heavy. She slips under the covers. I get in the bed and lift myself on top of her. When I kiss her she tastes like a lime margarita, salt around the rim. I let my body lean on her and I am surprised by how warm she feels. I put on a condom but am still half flaccid. I have to cup my penis in my hands and rub it against her until I'm hard enough to slip inside. When I do I shut my eyes and hide my face in her neck and the pillow. After we finish she lies with her back facing me and starts talking again.

"My daughter, Steph, wants a tattoo. She keeps asking me, and I told her I'd wring her neck if she gets one. Then I told her to draw what she wanted on herself for a month to see if she really liked it or not."

"That's a good idea," I say.

"Yeah, well, that's what I thought. Now she's covered in pen marks. She's always drawing on herself. She does little butterflies, and turtles and stuff. You know, stuff she'll hate in five years."

"What about this?" I say, running my hand down her side to the small of her back where there is a little tattoo outline of a bird in flight.

"Well, like I tell her, I know what I'm talking about. She

wrote a line from some poem on her forearm the other day, and I'm worried because this one has lasted all week. 'I will show you fear in a handful of dust,' it says."

"I'm not sure I know what that means," I say, thinking that this is something I could do. I could travel around my territory spending time with lonely women, finding bits of comfort to keep me from starving.

"I'm not sure she does either," Meredith says. "What does she know of fear?"

"'I will show you fear in a handful of dust,'" I say aloud while watching the side of Meredith's face. She has small lines spider-webbing out from the corner of her eye, and looks nervous and tired all at once. I run my hand over her tattoo again. "At least she's not jumping off buildings."

"Oh, he must get his wild side from you," Meredith says.

"I don't know about that."

Her hand runs over my forearm. "Haven't you ever done anything wild?" she asks me, and taps a fingertip against the faint dent below my eye where Lenwood Murry broke my eye socket in a childhood fight.

"I will show you fear as a long empty life," I say to her.

She lets her forehead fall on my shoulder like this was some old intimacy we had.

As we lie there I remember something that happened when I was Dennis's age. I had gone into the cemetery across the street from my parents' house with my brother, Lewis. The trees there were mostly black spruce, so the ground was covered in needles that felt soft beneath our feet. We had talked about hunting for opossums, and when it got dark that night we went out with flashlights. Lewis seemed to know what he was doing and after an hour of walking around the dark woods with our beams of light scanning the ground, gravestones, and canopy we saw a set of eyes reflecting back at us. Lewis put his light on it and it hissed at us showing four large fangs and a head full of long whiskers. I'd never seen one before. Its white face angled back from its pink nose and curved up into limp triangular ears that hung forward. I didn't even think about it when it happened, I just did what Lewis told me. With the opossum frozen in Lewis's beam, I ran toward it, bent down, and rapped it on the top of the head with my clenched fist, and then jumped away.

"Jesus, it worked?!" I heard Lewis say, his laughter breaking into surprise.

I looked down at the prehistoric-looking opossum lying motionless on the ground. Lewis's flashlight beam was shaking from laughing so hard.

It had never occurred to me this was something he hadn't done himself. I put my own light on the opossum and reached down and grabbed its hairless cord of a tail, thick like a rope of cartilage. I lifted its motionless body up. Lewis's beam of light steadied on me as I held it like a fisherman holds up his catch for a photo. That's when I saw the slow shifting of three little babies on the animal's back, and dropped it on the ground. Lewis jumped back from me and watched until the opossum rolled over and started slowly walking away.

The story became a demi-legend throughout my school days, and it was a small privilege to have such notoriety. The truth was, I was filled with regret over going along with what my brother said, for hitting that opossum's head, and then dropping those harmless animals.

In the morning Meredith gets up before I do, and wakes me after she showers and dresses.

"You going to come through town again soon, sailor?" she asks, leaning her knees on the bed, which sinks to her weight.

"Yeah," I say, and she leans over me and kisses my lips, then gets up and leaves the room.

My brother, Lewis, is an actual sailor, having gone into the navy and then spending his whole adult life as a merchant marine. I wonder if he's gone around the world seeking comfort with strangers like the sailor stereotype. I stay in bed looking at a dull watermark on the ceiling. I wonder who has been here before me, and where they kept their fear.

When I get home later in the week I drive to St. Francis to pick Dennis up from cross-country practice. The sports field spreads out behind the school. I park my car and walk around the building. There are ten boys running from the far field toward a man my age standing with a stopwatch. The man calls out times as the boys pass him and collapse on the ground after their last sprint. I don't see Dennis in the group when the boys start walking toward the building behind me.

"Where is Dennis?" I ask one of the kids I recognize as someone Dennis used to spend time with.

"I don't know," the boy says.

"Was he at practice today?" I ask.

"Umm—he's not on our team," the boy says.

I immediately feel foolish again, this time for having been duped by my son. I turn to my car and call his cell phone and then my house to see if he'll answer. Then I call Dyla's. Tom picks up.

"He isn't here," Tom says. "Should we be worried?" he asks.

"No, no—he's probably on his way to my place and I missed him," I say, then walk to my car.

I'll show you fear in an empty field.

I drive to Dennis's friend Adler's house, where I've dropped him off before. In the car I remember all the dark thoughts I used to have while Dyla and I were still married. Dyla would take Dennis out and they'd be gone too long after going out for ice cream or for a playdate. Drunk drivers. Semis not paying attention. My head a swarm of losses. I'd keep myself busy doing work on the house, or inventing some project to keep that possibility away. Sometimes I'd fast-forward through the initial phone call, the finding out, the grief, the years of recalibration to what my life would look like. I know it was some sort of perverse daydream but a similar feeling rises back up in me as I pull up in front of Adler's house.

No one answers when I knock, but I hear people in the backyard. I walk around the house and open the wooden gate. I'm about to call out hello, but I hear a bunch of voices start yelling as soon as I latch the gate shut behind me. When I turn the corner, I see that the yard is filled with teenagers. About thirty of them are circled up with their arms linked at the elbows. I walk toward them without one of them looking at me. Over their heads, in the middle of the circle, I see Dennis and Adler brawling, both topless, wearing makeshift boxing gloves made out of Ace bandages and athletic tape. They are striking each other cleanly in the face, and I'm amazed they are each withstanding the other's punches. I push my way through the link of bodies and wedge myself in between the two boys. My arms are spread out and my hands are pinned against the boys' chests like I'm timing their pulses.

"*Vhat* are you doing?" Dennis says. When I turn to him I see him talking through a mouth guard. "Dad, what are you doing?" he spits out. There is no fear in his eyes, which are bulging out, and his chest heaves up and down with each breath he takes. "We're not done yet," he says, furious at me now, his eyes wild. I look at Adler who is leaning into my other hand. His eyes are also testosterone wild. He has on maroon shorts with a little gold emblem of the Wolf of Gubbio on the right leg.

There are little red lights on the phones some of the kids are holding. I know that despite what they record, this moment will become a thing of folklore among these kids. It will become like the story of St. Francis and the wolf, converted into myth, and this story will grow, swell, and swallow what really happened until it settles like pond specks at the base of who my son is, and the type of person he can one day look back on as being— fearless, full of grace, wild, unabashed, and holy.

"Dad! Dad! Get out of our way," Dennis yells.

I'm not sure what it is in his voice that makes me look at him just then. I look right into his life, what it will be, and the odds that it won't be so much different than mine. This thought strikes me with an incredible empathy for him, as I know such moments of story-making are the only art some of us are given.

I put my hands down to my sides and step back from the boys like a referee.

"Okay," Dennis says to Adler. They hunker down, cock their arms, and let their fists fly at each other. And as I watch I think of the ancient-looking opossum I caught when I was a kid, pink like new and gray like old. A creature who must have instinctually known how to carry its children on its back.

11

Lewis Thurber, 2007

When he wasn't working, Lewis Thurber woke at 6 A.M. regardless of what time zone he was in. Sometimes he heard his name being called like a heavy whisper and would jolt awake. In Pattaya, Thailand, he walked down to the marketplace to eat tilapia and bean sprout spring rolls for breakfast, dipping the rice paper shells into small Styrofoam dishes of sweet red chili sauce until he was full. There was a stall that sold English newspapers and bitter dark coffee that he drank a quarter cup of before topping it back off with powdered creamer and sugar until it became thick and granular. In another stall he thumbed through the boxes of pirated DVDs and bought them to watch when it got too hot in the afternoons.

After leaving the market, he wandered the city. Blaring music and raging drunks spilled from the go-go bars, so he took the long way around the golf course to the Amari Nova tourist hotel and sat by the pool. Being white, Lewis was never questioned by the doorman as to whether he was staying at the hotel. A row of metal tables with round glass tops and wide canvas umbrellas were already opened and cocked toward the sun. In the shade he held the paper open to block out anything beyond the page, and read it cover to cover. When he finished he dived into the pool and did laps until his shoulders burned. He screamed under the surface so his words gurgled up the side of his head in a violent stream of bubbles. Then he flipped and floated on his back, taking deep breaths to settle back into his body. When he dried off he left the hotel and walked the beach, where the sky was blue and saturated with the sharp glow of the sun, then around the city until the heat was too much.

He had set his life to this schedule since getting off his last ship—a Dole banana cargo ship from Puerto Barrios, Guatemala, that ran up the western seaboard of the United States before heading for Asia and then back. He worked as a second mate for five months. On his bridge watches he was responsible for plotting the ship's course and prepping the navigational charts. He studied the navigation charts and liked to find where he was on that space. *I am here*, he thought. He did this enough that he began to think the world around him was a map that he could zoom out of for perspective. He'd rise over the physicality of his existence and the tide of emotions he'd spent years building levees against. It calmed him and made his troubles feel smaller. *I am here*. He'd pull out a larger chart. *I am here. I am here.*

Between watches he performed cargo checks to see if the cargo container's nitrogen systems were running properly. Each container had the oxygen sucked out and nitrogen pumped in to control when the bananas would ripen. One of the nitrogen compressors broke on his last crossing, and the bananas inside spoiled in the heat and the stench got so bad that Lewis used the crane on the superstructure to dump the three tons of rotten bananas overboard where they fanned out in the ship's wake.

He spent the last ten days wandering through Pattaya, its market, and into the park with its giant statue of a globe with a dog and a woman nursing her child sitting on top. Boyet, a Filipino crewmate who was his guide to the subculture here, told him the statue was a testament to the fact that women and dogs covered every inch of this place. Men were known to come from far and wide to act as deviant as they pleased, in a way they would never be permitted to anywhere else on earth.

Lewis believed Boyet was right about the statue. The bars were filled with young girls, and every afternoon there were mongrel dogs with dark earthen-colored coats sleeping beneath almost every parked truck. When it got cooler, they came out from the shade to beg or steal food. The female dogs knew, from a lifetime of being kicked, to jump out of the way and keep their distance. They tottered off with their sagging nipples swinging beneath them like dark raisins. The males were harder to come by, as they were too aggressive to sit and beg. So most were killed, run down by cars that swerved to hit them—something Boyet had said was reasonable, as there were never any cold winters to naturally kill them off.

One morning, while sitting on the patio of the room Lewis stayed in a mile outside the downtown area, and watching a pirated version of the documentary *Blue Earth* on his laptop, Lewis watched the dog he named Nipples dodge cars across the street, crossing over to his side of the road. She lived under the shed on the golf course. The dog's whole body was covered in greasy cowlicks, and she had bubbled-up black scars crisscrossing her upright triangular ears. She came closer now than she had before, so he went inside and got the bag of beef jerky he had been luring her with all month. He walked back outside and lobbed a strip of the mangled meat onto the grass. Nipples hunched forward and loped back toward the road after swallowing the meat whole. He threw her more until she was on the lip of the patio. Then he flung another piece inside the door to his room. When she went for it, Lewis pushed the door shut between them and locked her inside.

He sat in front of the glass on his patio as if his room were a zoo display. The noise from the movie on the laptop crashed behind him. He tapped the glass, holding jerky in his hand, and part of him felt bent, perverse.

Nipples paced the far corner of the room with one side always touching the wall like a rat. She pivoted at the bathroom and again at the corner of the kitchenette where the slab of faux marble met curls of peeling blue wallpaper. Lewis slipped inside, blocking the opening to the door in case she tried to bolt. He flung another piece of jerky toward her and sat on the bare mattress of his bed. She grabbed it and resumed her stride as she chewed. He held the next piece in front of him.

"Here you go, girl," he cooed. When she didn't come any closer he dropped the jerky on the ground at his feet where it looked like a link of molted snakeskin.

Nipples skulked toward the bed and bowed her head for the meat. He reached his hand out. As his fingers grazed against the grain of her coarse fur she dodged her head and snapped her mouth shut over the center of his right hand. The dog's sharp stabbing canines sunk in deep behind his knuckles. As she yanked backward, her teeth scraped against his bones and he sprang off the bed and kicked her brindled chest. When she rolled backward his hand recoiled and droplets of blood flew against his face and landed on the mattress. A red bead sank into the cloth and set like an infant's fingerprint.

"I was just trying to pet you, you scrawny bitch," he said, lying onto the mattress and pinning his hand to his chest. There were fatty red tracks of exposed flesh torn back from his palm and the blood felt like warm milk soaking into his shirt as he stared at the ceiling fan trying to block out the pain. He tried remembering when he named her. He admired her protruding ribs as being a lean reflection of a scavenger's diet, a sign she would get by anywhere.

There was a tourist hospital in the new part of the city that could stitch him up and give him a tetanus shot, but he figured it wasn't an emergency, and he could wait a bit.

"It's all right," he said to the dog. "We'll be friends yet." He cut the shirt he was wearing into thin strips with a pocketknife, wrapped the strips around the wound, and sutured the cloth together with lengths of duct tape. The fabric sponged up the blood, and he held the wadded-up hand over his head, and watched the dog shifting around his small room, which now smelled like it was wall-to-wall carpeted in dank fur.

He woke on the bed several hours later to Nipples scratching at the glass door. His bandaged hand was stained through and blackened with dried blood and his head was swimming as if he were a child in bed with fever again.

He got up and sat in the chair next to the window. It had gotten dark. He felt nauseous, and started smoking a Krong cigarette to settle his stomach. The drift of smoke blew through the crack in the sliding glass door like a slow river. The laptop was still on the patio table. He was surprised the screen was playing the *Blue Earth* intro of a school of fish bunching up into a swirling silver fist. He liked watching their hypnotic movements and imagined what went on beneath the ocean, as it looked endless and empty from the surface. On late-night watches he read books about the millions of fish beneath the vessel. The complexity and diversity humbled him. When he read about mouthbreeding, where some males will take their newly hatched young into their mouth to keep them safe, he felt a little nauseous imagining little fish fluttering against the inside of his cheek.

He watched the screen until he was distracted by a pack of vacationing US Navy men who descended on the golf course across the road. They screamed and tackled one another on the greens and rolled around in drunken revelry. One took the sand rake above his head, and began digging a hole beneath the spongy surface. Another grabbed the pin flag and heaved it like a javelin so far that the orange triangle flag fluttering behind it disappeared into the night. They chased after it with the same torrent of energy that brought them and ran down the road toward the bar district.

Since finishing his own tour with the navy more than ten years ago, and all the time afterward working as a merchant marine, Lewis came to recognize the ships as floating dens of horny men who operated under different moral standards when they came ashore. Most of them idealized women in their own twisted ways. The captain aboard his last ship, Russell Bartuga, had a tattoo of a naked angel with glorious wings and sweet blue-tipped breasts draped over his forearm. Once, during the night watch, he told Lewis that he liked to take girls to his room and make them wrestle with him. Then he put a pillow over their heads and punched the pillow while they were having sex. It was as if something happened to the hearts of people who were always alone at sea, such that they no longer knew how to open up to others, leaving only an ill-aligned organ at the center of their chests. Lewis worried he was finally turning into one of them— the lonely men who slipped ashore to buy and sell what they needed—coming back looking consecrated and free of something, as if only raw and carnal experience could shock their hearts to beating.

When Lewis wasn't working he felt disorientated. Life on the ships was regimented, spelled out, and the problems he learned to protect against were tangible and immediate. He liked that—liked how many different ways there were to call for help at sea, how specific you had to be to send out SOS signals. If the ship was on fire or taking on water you held down your foghorn, fired a gun at one-minute intervals, shot your flares, and transmitted your position while calling "Mayday, Mayday." He liked having so many ways to call for help there, because on land he could think of none.

After the navy guys ran off, he locked Nipples in and walked down the same road they had, north to the tourist strip. The muggy air filled the space between his bandage and the cut and everything in his arm was throbbing. The pain was making him feel sick. He expected more navy boys to pass him on the road at any time. Sailors knew to save their money on lodging and stay outside of the tourist strip so they could spend it all in the clubs.

He stopped at a small oceanfront bar called Tynig-Jata; maybe some food would make him feel better. He ordered a large dish with peanuts, sliced limes, chopped ginger, fresh peppers, garlic, and mango that was scooped up and wrapped in lettuce leaves. The restaurant looked out onto the distant water, where waves were frozen at their crests. As he ate, the city around him grew darker. Fierce colors began pulsating from all the shops, angry reds and burning oranges until the place was alive with the richness of its own natural beauty colliding with the dirty streets and neon bar signs.

There was a monthly Thai boxing match about to start in the back of a go-go bar that Boyet had told him he had to see. After he ate he walked past a pale gray concrete Catholic church and a bathhouse where nude women stripped off your clothes and scrubbed your body with soft, fat sponges. The streets threw off a great heat and the briny scent of fried meat, ginger, and burning trash floated through the air near the waterfront where fishing boats anchored at night. As the streets narrowed and became more crowded the racket of locals calling to each other under the flushed light of the store awnings cluttered up and grated on his aching head.

When he got to Nan's Luck Bar, a dark-haired Thai man with an unlit, half-spent cigarette hanging from his lips sprang off a swivel barstool and met him at the door.

"Hello, my friend," he said. "Come, come in."

Lewis followed him to the back of the bar, where a doorframe was covered in a bead curtain. The man's black silk shirt had an electric-green tiger embroidered across the back that swayed across his shoulders as he walked through the curtain into a warehouse-size room with a small ring surrounded by tables that were already full.

"Come, come in," the barman said. "You want seat for the show?" The man hooked the palm of his hand around Lewis's elbow and led him to a small table four rows back from the ring. A busload of male Japanese tourists filled the front rows of tables. There were other foreigners in the crowd. Asians, Arabs, and a few white men from around the world from what he could tell. Scattered around the bar were bored-looking girls wearing short, formfitting, one-piece dresses and glossy black or red high heels. In the ring there were already two fighters circling each other and colliding with knees, elbows, fists, and long graceful swings of their feet. Lewis heard a loud slap of the fighter in blue trunks landing a kick against the glove-protected head of his opponent followed by a chorus of rising yells from around the ring.

"Good view for fight," the barman said, the burned tobacco end of his cigarette rising and falling from his lips as he spoke.

"This is great," Lewis said.

"You watch fight. I'll get you drinks first. What you like now?"

"A Singha lager and three shots of strong vodka on the side."

"Very good," the barman said, and left Lewis at the table. The rafters of the bar were painted in smoke. The only people standing in the room were the fighters and girls walking between tables and running their fingertips across the shoulder blades of random men.

"You want to bet on fights?" the barman asked when he came back with Lewis's drinks. "I'll bring you lines on fight card if you like."

"That would be fine," Lewis said. The barman spun away and went out through the curtain. Lewis loosened the tape and T-shirt bandaging around his wrist and poured a shot of vodka down the inside of his hand. Then he spun his hand over and poured the second down the outside before he swallowed the third. The shot warmed his chest and stomach and eased the sting of the liquor flowing over the puncture marks from Nipples. He shut his eyes and let a series of slapping sounds from the ring, the smell of the smoky bar, and the vodka's twinge at the back of his tongue settle.

"Hell of a fight, oi," an Australian man sitting at the next table leaned over and said. Lewis nodded to him and turned back to the ring. "These two here have been going at it for six rounds already," the Aussie said. "It's one of the best fights I've seen."

On ships Lewis met people from all over the world, and on the long watches or during meals, they told stories to pass the time, but never shared anything too honest or real. The generic language of stories was the language of the sea and Lewis heard the sea when the Aussie asked, "Care to join me?"

"Ah, good. You have friend," the barman said, putting a fight card in front of Lewis. "You guys want some girlfriends now—huh? Or ladyboys?"

"That's right. Euclid here will take care of us," the Aussie said, and squeezed the barman's butt cheek. He said something in Thai to him, to which the barman nodded and walked away.

"You been in long?" the Australian asked Lewis.

"A bit over a month now," Lewis told him, yelling over the crowd.

"You feeling all right, mate?" the Aussie asked looking at the bloodied makeshift bandage on his hand that was now dripping vodka onto the floor.

"Yeah, I'm getting there," Lewis said.

All the men in the bar seemed desirous of everything at once and were either yelling at the ring or flirting with the girls Euclid had shuffled into their laps. On the table in front of him Euclid had placed a match card with a long list of names and odds written by hand next to each set of fighters.

"This is a pretty wild place," Lewis yelled to the Aussie.

"Isn't it great?" the Australian yelled without taking his eyes off the ring. The fighters were leaning into each other, embracing, and swinging their knees high and wide into the flexed abdomens of their opponents. The Aussie yelled out something in Thai and a troubling sense of weightlessness came over Lewis, knowing he still hadn't found a place in the world he understood or could call his own.

Lewis had been eighteen when he joined the navy. At the time he did not comprehend that going to sea would open the whole world up to him like an ugly flower and take him to all the places he'd only read about. That on leaves between contracts there would be no one telling him what to do and his time would have to be filled doing something else. That eventually he'd go to ships and feel at home, and go on leave and feel lost again. That that would become the simple rhythm of his life.

The bell rang to end the round, and both fighters went to their corners.

"Oh, here we go. This will be good, mate," the Aussie said and pointed to the bead curtain at the entrance of the room.

A naked girl was walking into the room, and the bead strings rolled off her shoulders and swung back to the clattering tangle of the curtain. The girl took a running step and dived under the bottom rope and slid chest first onto the stained ring mat. She was no more than twenty years old and she made a show of sitting down so her bare ass hit the ring's canvas with her legs spread akimbo and her hands behind her back. Then she brought one hand forward, and the Japanese men at the front all seemed to inch closer on their chairs when they saw the downy yellow duckling she raised over her head. Lewis's stomach heaved up a vodka-bile taste as he glanced from the girl to the men.

The girl leaned back onto the canvas with her legs spread wide, brought the duck down, and cupped the bird against herself. Her face turned red as her hand inched the duck back and forth until it was inside of her. There was a cacophony of different languages yelling at her and to each other around the ring. The sounds corkscrewed into something clattering and confusing in Lewis's mind and he tried to focus on anything audible coming from the girl, but she didn't make a sound.

Lewis reached for his wallet, grabbed a handful of cash with the fingers sticking out of his wrapped hand, and tossed it on the table. The girl in the ring lifted both her empty hands and waved them in front of her like a hand model. Nothing in the bar seemed to be a part of her world as she lifted her pelvis off the ground and got into a squatting position with each hand resting on a bent knee. As Lewis turned to walk away he saw from the corner of his eyes the dark little bulge of the reemerged duckling fall out and drop free. It landed on its side, hopped up and waddled straight toward the front row, where one man emerged from the crowd and grabbed it.

"You like?" Euclid asked, standing next to Lewis again. "You can take her with you when she is done if you like." Lewis brushed past him. "We have others too. Come, come, we'll see," Euclid said and grabbed Lewis by the arm and pulled him toward the back side of the bar.

"Was this the last fight?" Lewis asked.

"No, no. We have many more."

"Do you always have intermissions like that?"

"Yes. We have lots of great shows with the girls. Come, come, I'll show you more girls you take home."

Lewis wanted to get a cold drink and to forget what he had seen. He looked closely at Euclid's face as if he expected to see the green tiger climb over the man's shoulders and swipe at his jugular.

The smell of old beer and new smoke were churning up from the sticky floor as Euclid led him to the bead curtain. Behind him was not the last fight, but one in a line that he knew would never end.

On the other side of the curtain Euclid led him through a door he had not noticed when he first entered.

"Come, look what nice girls I have for you." The door opened into a small room full of couches. Inside were six girls. "Go in the back," Euclid said to a pregnant girl. Her shoulders sloped over her fecund stomach. Two of the women on the couches had to help her stand up.

"I'll take her," Lewis said.

The pregnant girl looked nervous when Lewis pointed to her.

"Oh, good choice my friend. This one, very special," Euclid said.

"I'll take her," he said again, pushing a wad of American five-dollar bills into Euclid's hand so he could get out of there as quickly as possible.

Lewis broke back into the street with the pregnant woman at his side. As she walked, her arched back pushed her stomach forward. Her sable hair parted in the middle, hung over her shoulders, and rested above her swollen breasts. The blue neon light from the neighboring bar reflecting off her black eyes reminded him of Sterno flames. To his right the main drag of go-go bars ended at the ocean. The shore smelled like something wilted on the edge of a vast and dying place and only accelerated his encroaching sickness. An airplane was moving across the darkness. The streets were so lit up he thought of what it must look like to people looking down on the city—their foreheads pressed against serving plate–size windows as they dropped out of the clouds to view all the lights and wonder what heathen festival awaited their descent. He imagined lighting his vodka-soaked hand and waving it above his head to guide the plane down.

They walked back toward Lewis's place along the water. There were new streamline cargo ships and dirty old freighters slowly rocking offshore. He wished he were out there. In the total darkness of open water he had seen Orion throw his leg over the horizon and climb the sky, stars dripping off his shoulders and pooling into constellations of animals and heroes impaling each other in the heavens.

The woman had to stop every hundred yards. Perspiration beaded below her hairline, which reminded him of his first time in a brothel, where the sweat on a whore repulsed him, as that sweat might have been worked up from having serviced the ship that came in before his. It hinted at something fluid and human that had always made him uncomfortable.

His hand started to pound, so he held it in front of him like a boxing glove made out of a wadded-up diaper. His fever was getting worse, and he not only felt sick, but on the strange streets with the quiet pregnant woman, he also felt ugly and sick of himself.

She was probably eighteen or nineteen, and he thought Euclid said her name was Rena.

They stopped at the headlands and he smelled the water. He shut his eyes and listened to the breakers that will come until the end of time. When the woman was ready to walk again he opened his eyes and scanned the sky for satellites cutting their straight lines across the stars.

"You American?" she asked.

"Yes."

"You work ship?"

"Yes."

"Lots from ship come to Pattaya," she said.

"Yes, lots."

She pushed her hair off her collarbone, and as it swung loose he tried conjuring an odd want for her.

"No one knows you," she said.

"What?"

"No one knows you," she said again, this time pointing to the buildings, as if suggesting the whole world beyond them. "No one—" She searched for another word as she waddled forward.

Across the street was the golf course cut from the jungle

with a long fairway sloping to the ocean. From his patio, when it was light out, he could see the broken lines of cresting waves gathering at the curve in the beach.

"I mean no family? No one knows you?"

"Oh. No," he said. Though he did have a family. His father doggedly wrote him once a week. One of the letters had a picture of his mother and father before any of the kids were born. They were leaning shoulder to shoulder against the side of a rusted red VW Bus and smiling. They were just kids. The whole world ahead of them. The big family to come. The upheavals. None of that yet hinted at on their bright faces.

In another letter, his father sent a Polaroid of Lewis with Connor and Jamie as small kids. All of them were in motion, darting toward the corners of what the lens could capture. Too wild to sit still for even an instant. The photo had dark smudges in the bottom-right corner on the front and back where it was worn from holding. He imagined his father studying this picture, trying to trace the shifting energy of his children.

Over the years in some port calls, dozens of those letters had stacked up. His nephew, Dennis, was born while Lewis was sailing in the South China Sea. His niece, Tina, when he was crossing the Indian Ocean. He called his siblings from a satellite phone on the bridge each time. There were still those distant connections. And he still felt the dull thump of love for them that persisted despite the time and distance and silence that existed between them. He could now see his dark patio window and watched for a flash of Nipples pacing the room. His room was a dump compared to the tourist hotels but he could afford to stay on this side of town for as long as he wanted.

The room cost 160 US dollars a month. Rena had cost 30 dollars for the evening. Her words played in his head again. "No one knows you."

He brought Rena to the long hallway of other rooms, and she waited as he opened the door slowly so Nipples couldn't flee. Once inside he looked closely at the urine-colored mattress on the bed. When he shut the door, Rena stepped farther into the room. She was obscenely large for her small frame, with tan, fat ankles slipping out of leather sandals with soles made of cut-up tire rubber.

As soon as she saw Nipples, Rena's red-rimmed eyes flashed to Lewis. Nipples went to the far corner of the room and curled up with her head resting on her tail.

"You like dogs?" Rena asked.

"Yes," he said.

"Is your dog?" Rena was looking around the room and flashing looks at Lewis's wrapped hand.

"She's my friend," Lewis told her.

"You like big ladies too?" she said and patted her splayed hands against her belly.

"Yes," he said. Nipples was looking at them from the kitchenette. Lewis stepped toward Rena. He expected her to say something to him, to ask him to be gentle with her, but she didn't. She looked at him with a sexy, pouty look he was sure she had been trained to give to men her entire adult life. He wanted her to say something. He had wanted the girl with the duckling to say something too—some small hint of outrage.

Because he didn't know what else to do, he reached his hand toward her stomach but recoiled when a ghastly scream ripped in from the hall. Nipples jumped up and started barking. Lewis ran into the dark corridor that now felt tight as a grave. It was empty and he shut his eyes and listened, but all he heard was the sound of someone disappearing. He thought of Russell Bartuga punching his lover's pillow-clad face—swinging wildly to make sure someone on earth knew him and would remember him once he left.

Alone in the hallway he felt his heart furiously pumping in his hand and a dark part of him felt this was the kind of night he might actually welcome such a horror, such a visceral under-standing of life—if only for an instant.

Rena was leaning against the sliding glass door when Lewis walked back into his room. He knew if he slid the door open, both Nipples and Rena would run into the darkness and he'd be left in his lonely room with nothing to distract him from his need. So he crossed the horrible carpet, toward Rena, who turned away and made the sign of the cross—maybe asking for him not to damage her baby or for some kind of redemption, for her God or Jesus to turn a blind eye for the next hour, and he understood what made her do it, as he wanted redemption too, though it wasn't anywhere at hand.

While she was facing away from him, he wrapped one sweaty and one bandaged hand about her stomach and pressed himself hard against her, and then led her away from the glass door. Neither of them talked. The fingertips of his good hand ran under the strap of Rena's dress and pushed it over her shoulders until it hung on by her breast and stomach. As he led her to the bed she was mouthing something—a prayer. The bible would do nothing for them here. Maybe he could make up his own bible. A reading from the book of Tides: And ye shall be washed ashore, and pulled back to sea naked and renewed.

He laid her back on the bed, kneeled between her legs, and brought his mouth between her thighs. Rena's skin tasted like the exposed top of a battery washed in lavender soap. Nipples stood up next to him and started nervously sniffing the bed as if to test the timbre of the woman's whimpers—searching out what was really in her heart or body. The image of himself made Lewis think that the world was full of people balancing on the fulcrum of tenderness and danger.

When Rena's voice started ululating higher and louder he stopped but her legs rose off the ground and her soft calves wrapped around the back of his neck. She arched her body backward when she came, and the bulbous bottom of her stomach pressed against Lewis' forehead. He sat back and crawled onto the bed, scooping his arms under her so she could shimmy the rest of her body onto the mattress. Her naked body next to him sent a pang of loneliness through him. Then she reached for his waistline.

"No," he said, pushing her hand back toward the bed.

"That all you want?" she asked.

Lewis lay down next to her, clutched her belly, and rested his left ear against her popped navel as the room grew darker around him. After several minutes, something pressed briefly against his cheek, and he held her tighter until it pressed again. Rena's hand came down and rubbed through his hair as he felt the fetal churning of her child, some bastard child of a Filipino sailor, a freighter messman off for leave in the dock towns, having long forgotten about her. He presumed if this child were a girl, she, too, would know plenty of lonely men off the ocean seeking some immediate fix.

The baby kicked again. "It's a duck," he whispered, holding tighter to her stomach as if afraid to fall off the bed, fully aware now of some sadness that had been on the verge of release.

Rena's hand pulled back his bangs and each finger slowly worked its way over his scalp. As he lay with her, he imagined her unborn child growing up the destitute offspring of a whore, sucking on an overused nipple. He imagined the child picking among the trash for food, trying to give names to the things she would think were myth and magic, and as he was falling asleep, he imagined giving her a new path and carrying her away.

Then something pulled him awake. He tried to fight it, but opening his eyes he saw the last wrappings of his mummified bandage being pulled off his hand by Nipples. Enough light was shining through the curtain that he knew it was six in the morning, and he felt like he'd just come alive again after a long sickness—a nightmare finally lifting. Rena was gone, and Nipples was licking the crust of dried blood away from his hand. He opened his palm to the animal's warm tongue. The light traced its way from the far corner along the floor to the bed and up the ceiling. He felt the old longing for the steady work of ships and the sea—of having some job always waiting for him. The longing gave him some hope that he might still have a purpose and he started to feel a physical strength coming back to him. And stretching out each finger, he offered it all to the broken animal lapping at his hand.

12

Jamie Thurber, 2013

The wires running from small white suction cups on my head to the computer make little green lines on the screen jump up and down sporadically when Chow-Fung asks me if I know what the color mauve tastes like. When I tell him I don't, the lift and drop of the electronic lines seem to level out. I keep looking between him and the green lines as he asks me complex math equations, reads elementary alphabet books, and asks me to blurt out the first word that pops into my head when he says *sex*. He seems quite pleased with the whole process, intently running a metallic-looking pen over his notepad. He asks several odd questions that make me think he's privy to some faction of the world I have no idea about. I'm starting to wonder if this intense young man knows the feel of nothingness and the smell of sound.

He lets me take the suction-cup helmet off my head to use the ladies' room halfway through our three-hour session. In the stall, I wonder what my brain lines are casting as I hear a stream of pee hitting the water. The second half of our session requires me to be quiet after each question, letting my brain waves answer Chow-Fung.

"This is like how your brain works when sleeping," he tells me, pointing to the screen where the lines are still gyrating. "It's pretty busy up there all the time."

Chow-Fung is a doctoral student in educational psychology here at Buffalo State. I answered his mass email requesting volunteers for his study out of a combination of curiosity and a desire to meet people, a person, someone—anyone really. Everything about his demeanor is serious and he makes no mention of his work, grants, or life. The three-hour session in his laboratory is solely for gathering data. Resting my hands on my lap, I feel frumpy, like the sex questions are nothing he would associate with me. My clothes start to feel too tight, and it seems like the temperature in the room is rising. At the end of the hour, sitting quietly, letting my brain talk to his computer, I'm ready to shake my limbs loose and yell at him. Nothing particular comes to mind, just frustrated gibberish. See what that does to his screen.

The laboratory has a small office where he comes out to see me after we've finished the tests. The cinder-block walls are painted a sort of dull aqua green left over from the seventies, lending the room, despite being impeccably clean, a sense of staleness.

"Thank you very much for coming, Professor Thurber," Chow-Fung says to me as he walks into the room. "Now, I can offer you the ten dollars or a T-shirt for your time."

"Oh, I'll just take the T-shirt, please," I say, making him turn to dig around in a file cabinet against the wall. His pants have creases in the butt from sitting so long. He pulls out a white shirt folded like it would be at the Gap. Shaking it loose he holds it up in front of me, pressing the top seam against both my shoulders.

"There, that should fit you well," he says.

My hands graze his as I grab the shirt, but his face shows no recognition of having been touched. Spinning the shirt toward me, I read the black bold letters: *I've seen how my brain works.*

"Slowly?" my daughter, Tina, says to me when she reads my T-shirt as I walk into our apartment.

"Very funny, smart aleck," I tell her.

She mumbles something toward the television and doesn't look at me when I sit on the couch next to her. I find it hard reconciling that this person is my daughter. She's just turned thirteen and recently cut her fruit punch–colored hair short in the back like a boy's, leaving two long strands of bangs parted from the center of her forehead, wrapping her face like quotation marks. She has the same rounded features and healthy coloring she did as a newborn when I would stare at her for hours in a state of near worship. She's still pretty, but now comes across as tough and a bit scary. She smells like cigarettes, but I can't get her to admit to smoking, and I've never found anything in her room. She's wearing a metal-studded black leather bracelet, but it's her socks that worry me. She alternately wears either small girls' socks with frills on the elastic or multicolored knee-highs like a slutty school girl. The socks on her seem overly suggestive, and it scares me that despite her aggressive and dark clothing, she's begun working sex appeal into her life. She learned it from me, I have no doubt, though I don't show it off as much as I used to, or what's left of it at least.

"I had a brain procedure done today," I tell her, hoping

exaggeration will spark some recognition that I'm alive. "I was held for hours while they ran tests."

"Shut up, Mom," Tina says, still watching some sort of anime cartoon.

"I did," I tell her, lowering my voice. "Look at the suction marks on my temple," I say, pointing to my head.

When she shifts toward me the small orange cotton tassels hanging off her socks sway from her feet on the coffee table. Her eyes are almost black and when she was young I'd watch myself in them. "It may be serious," I say, wanting her to keep looking at me.

Later, I hear her talking on the phone with one of her friends. "My mom might have brain cancer," she tells whoever is on the other line. I think of whatever life she imagined herself having changing as she speaks the words. She won't ever tell me about those imagined lives, but I know she gets the compulsion to play out her future from me. I recognize it on her like it has climbed out of my mirror and draped itself over her, like Chow-Fung draped the T-shirt over me. Part of me wants to see how she acts toward me now before telling her my brain is fine—though it doesn't know the taste of mauve and the green waves spiked at the word *sex*.

When she is off the phone I go to talk to her. Tina is sitting down at a kitchen nook table doing homework. One of the light bulbs is out and the room is half in shadow leaving the lone light spotlighting her soft hair. I stop and stare at her. The room with her in it now looks like a piece of art, and I'm flooded with love for her. It seems there is no way to be anything but in love with her. The feeling makes me think of my parents loving me this way. Of course they did. Of course they did. Everything I thought they burdened me with suddenly seems to switch from their lack to something different. Something I couldn't see until now. A wash of forgiveness comes. There would be no knowing this feeling without looking at my girl in the half-light. I want to send all this love back in time to my parents when they needed it most. I want to send it forward to my girl when she will judge me. Backward and forward through time, I want to send all my love, which seems like an important enough revelation to change how I live the rest of my life. I don't disturb her and go to my room to get ready for teaching.

"What are you doin'?" Tina asks from the doorframe of my room, next to a faceless painting of a woman in white clothes levitating over a gravestone that I made when I was a young woman. She won't come inside, thinking that this demonstrates to me how one shows respect by staying out of other people's rooms— though we both know that when either of us is home alone the whole house is ours, every drawer rifled through and put back as best as possible.

"I'm getting my lesson plans ready for class tomorrow," I tell her. I have an Introduction to Philosophy class. I'm supposed to teach St. Augustine's vision of the mind to eighteen-year-olds who spend the class time text-messaging each other and don't even pretend to look at me when I'm talking.

"So when do you find out what the deal is?" Tina asks, leaning into the doorframe.

"I guess it will take a few weeks. But I wouldn't worry about anything for now. There's no sense worrying until we know something for sure."

"Well, I'm still going to go to Dad's this week if you don't need anything," she says, turning away from me, shyly now, like her gothic cloak can't cover everything she's not sharing.

My classroom is one of those big lecture halls with stadium seating. "St. Augustine believed the mind was the producer of infinite images," I tell the class to start my lecture. None of my students look like they care. The few ROTC soldiers in the classroom are sitting straight up, but their eyes are glazed over. "A person can imagine a mountain, a snow-capped mountain, a mountain with a goat on it, a mountain inside of another mountain. The possibilities of what the mind can produce are infinite. The mind therefore is the best model for God that we can find. God can also produce infinite things; though what God produces is tangible, Augustine believed, the mind nonetheless holds the same generative potential." I like the idea but it apparently has no effect on my class. I think about telling them that the mind casts squiggly green lines of all their thoughts, that the mind can become sick and generate tumorous growths, that I myself was in peril of those green lines casting some growth in my own skull, and that for homework we could all sit tight and wait on the results of my brain-study tests.

On nights when Tina stays with her father, John, I cook a quick dinner and spend the evening doing research in the campus library. Tonight, I'm chopping onions, green bell peppers, and celery to mix in with marinara sauce from a jar. I'll make enough to last until Tina comes back at the end of the weekend. It's easy for me this way, but I miss her. I miss her even though she's like a pensive cat, keeping one flank to a wall or an exit every time I'm around her. I halve the celery stalks and get lost in my thoughts with the rhythm of my knife crunching through the veiny green walls. Each slice sends out a little mist that I feel on my fingers and I'm not sure I hear the knock on the door until it comes again.

"Tina told me," John says when I open the door. "She came home and started crying."

But *this* is Tina's home, I think, still surprised my daughter has another life without me, surprised to find evidence of it here, now, on my doorstep.

"Jesus, why didn't you tell me?" he asks, limping forward and hugging me toward his chest. When he puts his arms over my shoulders they feel like heavy links of an anchor chain, pulling me down, lifting me up, and holding me suspended in his grasp. He hasn't hugged me since leaving me three years ago. We hardly even see each other anymore. Tina bikes across town or has him pick her up after school. He smells the same though. It's the smell I slept with and woke to before I finally washed all my sheets and clothes of him.

"So what's going on?" he asks. My cheek rests against him, and my nose sinks into the valley of his chest muscles. I feel his chin on my head and suddenly realize my hand is against his back, gripping it like a closed claw. His T-shirt sticks to my face where my tears are soaking in.

"It's okay," he says. "Tell me what's going on."

I sob into his warm chest, hating him for only coming now. I think of all the infinite images of mountains a person can conjure and how none of them are worth a damn for leaning into like this.

"It's okay, I'm here now," he says. "Let's go inside and talk about it."

"No, no," I say backing away from him, hoping some internal mountain will hold me. "I can't now, I'm busy."

"You have to tell me what's going on, babe," he says.

"Don't call me 'babe'!" I yell at him. "You can't come around now and call me 'babe'!"

"I'm sorry. Let's sit down and talk about this. Are you hungry? Can I make you some dinner?" he asks.

"I've already eaten, and I'm late for a meeting."

"Come on, Jamie, you don't have a meeting, just talk to me. Please." He seems so familiar standing there, and all I want is to crash into him again, let him hold me up like he used to before every fantasy life I played out with him shattered against the fantasies he chased after. Thinking about that I feel a dormant anger rise up and I don't want to look at him anymore.

"I have to leave, John. I'm late."

"Please tell me what these tests were all about," he pleads.

"I'm not really sure, to be honest. But I don't want to talk about it right now," I say, walking to the couch and grabbing my bag. "Now, you can walk me out if you like, but I'm leaving."

"We need to talk about this, Jamie. If not tonight, then tomorrow," he says, shutting the door behind us as I walk by him.

"I'm coming by tomorrow. I'll take you out and we can talk. Okay?" He says the last part slowly, like he's being deflated as I shut my car door on him.

The evening traffic rush is over, and I can't imagine what I'm doing. I'm not sure where my new penchant for sick games has come from. I catch a red fox in my headlights as I pull into the campus parking lot. It trots slowly toward a girl who's talking into a cell phone. "Watch out! Watch out!" I yell, but the girl doesn't hear me and the fox passes behind her by no more than a foot and runs away.

I can only get a few hours of work done after a slow start, and I can't shake the feeling that I've lost my mind and am traumatizing my daughter. Walking to the small coffee cart next to the entrance of the library, I see Chow-Fung leaning over a large table surrounded by notebooks and texts. I order two coffees and go to his table.

"Maybe this will help you get through all those books tonight," I say, placing the hot cup of coffee onto his table. He looks up at me uncomprehendingly. His thin dark hair is ruffled at the bangs where his hand was propping up his head.

"Oh. Hello, Professor Thurber," he says sleepily.

"Are you still trying to figure out the brain?" I ask.

"I'm not sure I'll have it all set by tonight, but this will certainly help, thank you," he says picking up the cup of coffee.

"Well, I hope my brain was a help. I mean I hope it meant something—those tests." I imagine unbuttoning my blouse and having the T-shirt he'd given me underneath, but I'm not wearing it. Just an overwashed bra with dead elastic that I'm not sure he'd care to see. I imagine taking his hand from his book and using his fingers to trace words over my stomach that would be on a shirt I could give him. I'd do it in cursive so his fingers spelled out *I've seen how your body feels.*

"Thank you for the coffee, Professor," he says. "Your participation was important to my study."

"And when do you get all your results in?" I ask.

"Oh, those will take a long time to figure out, but your participation was important," he says again, wanting to get back to his work.

"Those tests were important, huh? I thought so. That's what I told my daughter," I say to him as I walk away, disappointed I couldn't get him to talk more.

I spend an hour in the morning looking out the window, waiting for John to pull up. I try to return to how it felt to have his arms over my shoulders and the way his chin rested on my head. For a moment, it felt like when we were younger, when all that desire and chemistry had the potential to surge back up the way it did after he was injured, and then again on our trip to Mexico. It makes me mad how no one tells the truth about love. Or maybe no one really knows the length and breadth of it, with its weary middles, and surprising rejuvenations.

When John arrives, he doesn't see me watching from the window as he takes a deep breath, slowly letting it out, trying to work up a smile before he limps over and knocks on the door. I never understood how he could win at poker nights with his friends when he wears every emotion and thought on his body—like a mime. I take the same sort of deep breath before answering, and it surprises me how much I want to be in love with him again.

"Good morning," he says, not making a move to come inside, "I thought we could go to the park and have a bike ride."

"Since when have you been a bike rider?"

"Well, get ready and I'll show you something," he says.

It's almost noon when I walk outside to his truck and see the handlebar rising from the cab. Inside there is a maroon tandem bicycle.

"Who'd you have in mind when you bought this thing?" I imagine him with whatever woman he has now, and her looking closely at the muscles of his back as he pumps away on the bike. I'm suddenly jealous, remembering women have always loved John.

"I bought it hoping to get Tina to spend some time with me," he says.

"Hah! How's that working for you?"

"How do you think?" he says, smiling. "She laughed at me when I showed it to her, said it was a piece of junk."

"That sounds about right," I say. "Listen, John—"

"Wait, let's go out for a while, get some fresh air, and we'll talk later, okay?" In his truck he pats my knee, and the weight of his hand seems tremendous. He's probably horrified at the thought of me dying and leaving him full-time with Tina. Tina who has grown away from us so quickly that I know we are both terrified of losing her completely. I watch as he drives us along the main roads to the trailhead of the bike path. The path connects our two neighborhoods and the parking lot is right in the middle of our two places, like he'd purposely chosen neutral ground.

John steadies the bike while I get on it. The first few yards after he pushes us off are wobbly until he straightens us out. Over his shoulder and around me tree branches hang overhead, full of light from what is becoming a beautiful day. The trail goes into the woods and follows a shallow river with brown water-glossed stones. I can see the muscles on his injured side straining as he pedals. From my own handlebars, which are close to him, I lean forward and place my forehead against his back.

"So what's going to happen?" he says softly as he stops pedaling and we glide down the path.

"I really don't know," I tell him, feeling like I have some sickness in me that's kept me isolated for so long.

"Well, can you tell me what it is at least? I can't not know, Jamie," he says. I can tell how scared he is, and I imagine us loving each other again would feel like this. At the bottom of the hill he starts pedaling and I hear a rattle from our bike. A twig full of leaves is caught in the chain, and when he slows down at the top of the hill I hop off to pull it out. "Is it bad?" he asks getting off the bike from the other side so he can look at me.

"It's just a twig," I say, crouching to pull it away.

"Come on, tell me something," he says, leaning toward me, making the bike roll backward enough that the chain slips under my thumb and pulls it into the teeth of the chain wheel.

My eyes aren't shut when I scream, and John's face muscles slacken and drop from confusion. When I scream again he sees that my finger is caught and reaches over the bike frame to grab me, but this rolls the bike back again and a tooth grinds through my thumbnail and pinches tight to the bone. The sound doesn't seem like it is coming from me. John tries to walk around the bike, but any fraction of movement only grinds the tooth deeper into the bloody pink pulp beneath my nail and pushes the nail away from the skin.

"Hold still," he says, turning the pedal, which makes my

head fill with the same horrible sound that I know is my own screaming.

The metal tooth on the chain wheel grinds down farther still, and from my knees I scream at him, "No! No! Stop!" From the corner of my eyes I see two bikers twenty yards up the trail watching us. John moves the pedal again, and as I feel the metal sink deeper into bone I hate him again for everything I ever hated him for in the past. The image of him holding me at my doorstep last night ruptures into nothing, like we had never touched, leaving only pain and this ineffectual man staring down at me.

"Help!" the scream says. The bikers come toward us. A man and his son. The look on the man's face when he kneels next to me is patient and sad, like he was waiting to see if John could rescue me without the embarrassment of needing a stranger to do it for him.

"I'm dying," I yell at John, "and you can't do anything!"

"You'll be okay, honey," the man tells me. The boy watches without saying anything. "Hold the bike steady," he tells John.

"What's your name?"

"Jamie."

"Okay, Jamie. I'm Travis. Now, there's no way to do this that won't hurt, so we'll just get it over with, okay?" He puts a hand on my shoulder so I look at him. He is a young man, boyish, if not for a thick stubble. He's trying to be kind, and when he tells me to hold my breath, I do. He grips the chain around the wheel and pulls down, trying to slacken it. He whispers, "Now pull," and I do, letting the top part of the fingernail tear off and the pink bloody part come loose and throb in front of me like everything in the world is chiseling into the tip of my thumb. "There you go," he says looking at my hand. "You may need a few stitches but you'll be fine now."

John is watching as I'm on my knees crying. His shadow crosses the bike and lies on the ground at my side. I think of his shadow with a snowcap on it. I think of his shadow next to a goat, of his shadow within another shadow, and of a shadow in love. The air on my torn skin hurts, and seeing how so little can strip away what protects how raw we are makes me deflated and angry.

John lays the bike down and kneels next to me. "You're dying?" he asks. There is now very little left of the man who hugged me the night before, only the old hurts that keep coming back, like our tangle of emotions are married, like there's another set of vows that were meant to last forever and ever, Amen.

"Do we need to go to the hospital?" he asks.

"No, I don't think more tests will do me any good. I'm going to go home. You can take your bike back for one of your girlfriends," I say, walking away from him.

"Jamie," he says, starting to walk after me.

I turn back toward him and hold out my good hand. "You can't help me, John. I thought you could. I wanted you to be able to, but you can't. I want to walk home by myself now."

People are biking and jogging past me on the trail going in both directions. In the sunlight they look happy. I wrap my fingers over my thumb and squeeze so it won't bleed anymore and I can't look at it. I walk past a small park with a playground and several winding bright yellow slides and a set of monkey bars. I catch the silhouette of a woman swinging from one bar to the next, a small boy jumping around beneath her saying, "You're almost there. Almost."

Several hundred yards past the playground there is a large corrugated iron train bridge. Through a cropping of bushes I see a group of kids ahead of me on the trail that dips under the bridge. There are over a dozen of them and I wonder who's supposed to be watching them.

I recognize an obese Latino kid with his shirt off from Tina's school and realize all these kids are skipping class.

"You ain't got the balls," the boy says, reaching under the fold of his gut and making a cupping motion on his crotch. "You ain't got the balls," he yells again, looking up to a group of six kids walking across the track to the middle of the bridge.

Tina walks onto the bridge slowly behind the group that is now in the middle looking down at the water. I stop behind the bush and am furious at her for skipping school. I figure if I wait a minute I can catch her smoking and pile up the charges on her. I see her lift her dark shirt up over her head. She's wearing a plain white bra, and I'm amazed as she slips her hands into the waistband of her skirt and pushes it down around her ankles and then walks to the group of kids on the bridge. From where I am I can see the small fold between her legs through white lace underwear, the two dots of her nipples, darker against the cotton cup of her small bra, the subtle arch of her stomach and shoulders, and the sun on her hair and round face. I used to have skin like that, I think, taking a giant step toward her, but I hear the voice again, "You ain't got the balls," and I can't bring myself to walk anymore; I'm frozen and can almost feel the air right around my daughter standing on the bridge.

She slips a leg through the wire cable of the bridge and the world slows down. She is so confident and beautiful it seems she should always be above others, so they can look up at her. She grips the cable behind her and leans forward. All the air in my chest sucks in on itself. The river I've been walking along can't be deeper than two feet, but I can't bring my feet to move. I want her to hold on tighter, to crawl back onto the bridge and go to school. I want to hold her, and for her to be able to fly if she falls.

I imagine my test results coming from Chow-Fung. I now know what they will say. They'll tell me the cord between the heart and the brain is taut. The brain or mind can do nothing but produce endless images that the heart, a first-class sucker, can only hope are true. But a lifetime of hoping for those images that never happen coats a person in a fine powder of disappointment, layer upon layer, until there is a heavy feeling of something solid and permanent that can't be chipped away. I watch Tina, who now seems to have all my qualities that are fading, and I want her to stay suspended above others without ever falling.

I look out from the bushes at my only child on the edge as she leans back into the bridge cables, bends her knees, and jumps. The bush scrapes my face as I dart out toward Tina who's just jumped into the mouth of disappointment, daring it to swallow her.

Waving both my hands over my head like I can catch her, I see the sound of the giant splash where Tina hits the water. I taste the smell of churned-up river water as her head comes up and shakes out her hair. Every inch of the world that holds and lifts my daughter is confused as she pops above the surface. I see her smile sink when she sees me running toward her. Her friends are all looking at me, too, like I am her crazed mother, or their own crazed mother, or the world is full of mothers lurking behind bushes waiting to charge them. I watch the water flow off Tina's shoulders as she scuttles out of the river and I can hear the yelling, I know they can all hear it, before I recognize the loud voice as my own. "I'm fine—I'm fine—I'm fine," the voice rings out, like it's understood I'm speaking for us all.

13

Lewis Thurber, 2018

Lewis felt wiggling fat rolls bunched from his waistline to his clavicles as he pedaled up the long incline. A slow heat burned from his quads to the bone with each strained pump of his legs. *Top of the rise, fat ass* had been his mantra for the last half hour on the hill. He'd rest at the top. He'd make it to the top. His neon-green jersey, frothed in sweat, stuck to his chest. His chest jiggled, and the bloom of embarrassment with how bad of a shape he was in since he'd begun studying for his captain's license made him pump his legs harder. When he crested the hill, he saw the long red-and-brown roll of Wyoming topography stretching out beneath a perfect blue sky. The sun glinted off the deep draws and rounded stones of dried creek beds on his glide down. With the wind whistling through his red helmet and panniers, he felt like he'd found a long-lost thread of a path he'd veered from that lay across the barren part of the country.

Now that he was in the West, inland, away from everything

at sea where he had built a life, he still couldn't describe it. The unassailable purity of the blue sky gave him a peace he had longed for, had known he had been missing for years. One truth was that he had become a soft, pink mess of a middle-aged man, overweight, prediabetic. Another, the one that mattered here, was that he felt very close to rediscovering some inner fire that used to drive him.

Several more large hills. Two he had to stop and push his bike on. Three long, fun descents. Then he found himself pedaling through rolling granite terraces that stretched out of sight. By his map, he was nearly two hundred miles from the old Motel 6 parking lot in Cheyenne he started from three days ago. By the same map, that left nearly seven hundred more miles to go. It seemed such an unobtainable distance. He set his next short-term goal as a town called Natrona, ten miles ahead. When he disembarked his last ship in Delaware the American shad, which traveled in large schools out at sea, were still making their runs, taking one flooded channel after another to get back to the river where they were spawned. The shad don't eat on their run home and live off their own fat, as if winnowing down to meet their pasts. The thought made him consider pushing off his meal but instead he ate a tortilla wrap full of peanut butter and drank a pint of water.

When he reached the sign, it read "Natrona, Population 16." He could envision it on a topographical map. *I am here.* All he saw was a train depot with a rusted diesel locomotive and a square, timber building with lacquered horizontal boarding and a red neon Budweiser sign. There was no name on the bar. A line of sparrows perched on the lip of the roof. In the gravel lot were two pickup trucks with souped-up suspensions and tires and a military-green heavy truck.

When he walked in the bar, the bottom of his bike shoes click-clacked against the olive-green faux-marble floor. A distorted mirror panel rose above the shelf with glasses, and the warped reflection made Lewis's eyes water. Two older men, each with blue mesh baseball caps curved in tight at the corners, sat at the far end of the bar. The men wore faded denim bib-and-brace overalls. A frumpy woman with teased auburn bangs, wide-waisted Dickies-blue slacks, and a V-neck T-shirt that showed off the tops of her enormous, low-slung breasts, stood behind the counter. Lewis sat on a stool. The cracked leather felt hard against his sweaty bike shorts. His bike clips clanked against the foot rail.

"Hello," he said.

The three people didn't turn toward him.

With his spandex suit and tight neon-green jersey, his gray hair helmet-molded to his scalp, and the *clip-clop* of a rotund Baryshnikov, he was surprised they weren't gawking at him.

"Excuse me, ma'am," Lewis said, raising a finger to the bar.

The woman didn't look away from the two men. None of them were talking.

The old man closest to him had what looked like a gin and tonic in front of him. Lewis imagined his finger dipping into and stirring the ice cubes in that drink. Licking his finger. Sucking on it. Then came that old desire to slip his skin and run wild through the night, inhaling booze, palming the cold sweat off of the glasses, blacking out, and shoving into strangers, wanting to sleep with or fight them.

"Excuse me," Lewis said again.

She turned and walked toward him. Her reflection curved and swelled as she walked the length of the mirror.

He wanted to order a cold beer, a six-pack of cold beers, but he knew that was Fat Lewis talking, Fat Lewis craving calories he burned over the last three days of biking. "May I please have a water and a can of tomato juice?" He even hated his order.

"We don't have tomato juice."

"That there will do fine," Lewis pointed to the little cans of tomato juice sitting next to the chrome coffee urn behind the counter.

"We don't have tomato juice," the woman said again. Her eyes were pinched, and even in the dim light, Lewis could see the shadow of a sickness beneath her skin. Cancer. ALS. Scurvy, for all he knew, as her lips didn't part when she spoke.

"Well. Do you serve any food?"

The two men at the end of the bar were looking at him now. Hard faces. One mustached, the other lined with deep-set wrinkles brimming with salt-and-pepper stubble along the jawline.

"Register's broken," she said. Light from the red Budweiser sign found little puffs of space in her hair and swirled there as she shifted in front of Lewis.

"Well, can I pay for anything in this fine establishment?"

"There's a little shop a few miles up the road you can spend money at."

The men at the end of the bar were unflinching. The woman's gaze sharpened.

"A few miles up is all," she said. Her lips stayed locked together.

"I have cash."

"Just a few miles."

"Well. Thanks for the hospitality," Lewis said, suppressing his urge to demand a bag of chips from behind the counter and yell, *You're a bunch of cracked-brain yokels.*

He eyed the fun-house mirror image of the bar, these out-of-the-way people, and the twisted version of himself. He liked what he saw, this other version of himself. At all other moments of his life, he would have turned and walked from the bar. He could see himself doing it and it made him angry. That was what Fat Lewis who ate three candy bars a day would do and he knew it. So he pulled a flip phone from his jersey's zipper pocket at the small of his back. There were no reception bars. There had been none all day. He tapped the phone on the bar and pretended to dial. He made a show of putting it to his ear.

"Yeah, Connor. Yeah, it's me," he said to no one. He kept his eyes locked on the three people in the bar. Do it, he urged himself. "I'm at that dump you told me about in Natrona."

All three of the strangers turned toward him now.

He paused, surprised by what he was doing. But he liked the oddity of the moment and knowing that in these wide-open spaces there was still room for him to be a different person. He could not only change his body but how he acted.

"Yeah. The place is crawling with mice like you said. Go ahead and file your health inspection report with the state." Lewis grinned at the closemouthed bartender. "Okay. Bye." He clicked the phone shut, peeled his wet bottom from the seat, eyed the two wet crescents of sweat left behind, and click-clacked out.

In the parking lot he sat by his bike for a moment and let

his nerves settle. He'd surprised himself with his fake call and was happy to have done so. As an act of owning what he had just done, he didn't start pedaling away. He stood where he was and ate another peanut butter burrito, washed it down with a pint of water, then sat back on his bike. His undercarriage was raw and sore from where the seat pressed into his bottom. He started biking farther north. The road was lined with meadow foxtail and white clover.

At any moment, he expected a truck to come up the road and run him down.

It was strange how quickly he thought of using his brother's name in the bar. He had not talked with Connor for years now, but as he strained to pedal up the next hill, the clear vision of his brother as a boy came to him. He and his brother were inseparable as children. They were tyrannosaurs, bent at the waist, elbows tucked to their ribs, forearms swatting at everything as they careened through the dining room. They dug shovel-blade-deep holes in the backyard looking for arrowheads; split rocks with hammers, hunting for trilobites. They tied D batteries together with lengths of twine and lassoed each other's feet. Taped the same twine to the doorway of their sister's bedroom and tied it to an alarm clock and pretended it was a trip-wire bomb, jumping out of her closet and making exploding noises as she toppled.

Lewis could see how there was a false summit to the hill ahead, but the peak would not be much farther beyond that. He had not thought of his own childhood in years but so much was sitting there now for him to find. He and Connor were headless horsemen, Zulu warriors, Union soldiers, and Blackbeard during the golden age of piracy. They gathered facts: tallest mountains, longest rivers, first pilots to fly an airplane. They shared these facts with people at random. Sang a song that named the fifty states but could not finish, trailing off after distant Idaho.

He cleared the false summit and felt the sting of remembering how he and his brother knew more than they should have about their parents' marriage. They had heard their fights and lovemaking and noticed how palpable with worry one seemed to make the other. Connor suspected they communicated in secret ink, their own complex, hidden code the kids had yet to break. He and Connor had hunted through their parents' room with a mail-order cipher wheel, looking to crack secrets open. They had kept busy to avoid the tension thick between their mother and father.

He and his brother were wild together. Their energy endless. Their memory together as children was fuel enough to fire him over the crest of the hill, where exhausted, he coasted downhill at faster and faster speeds so that the wind howled over his thoughts of such a long time ago.

Miles from the yokel bar, he rode with the noon sun into a valley with a large gable-roofed house, a corrugated sheet barn, and a flat-roofed building with a sign painted on the side that read "Bookstore." When he got closer, there was a split rail fence running the length of the property with a posted sign on every third post.

He'd felt good about what he'd done at the bar, and the idea of not being such a rule follower made him want to crack the day open in new and interesting ways. He rode onto the gravel driveway and leaned his bike against the fence and began walking up toward the house. The bookstore building was locked.

"Didn't hear anyone pull up," a woman's voice said behind him. She wore wire-rimmed glasses and a paint-stained denim smock. "I can open that for you if you like."

"Oh, hello there. I don't want to trouble you. I thought I'd take a breather."

"No trouble," she said. "You on a pedal bike?"

"Yes. At least until I get run over."

"Well, that's impressive. Don't get many of you. Or, any of you, to be honest."

She pulled a key from her pocket and worked it into the lock. When the door swung open she hit a light and he could see the inside was full of bookshelves, each almost seven feet tall, and two books deep on musty shelves that bowed under the weight.

"Whoa," Lewis said. "This is unexpected." The musty scent and old joy of bookstacks settled over him. He'd been a voracious reader ever since he broke into his father's storage unit looking to steal fireworks as a kid and found a lifetime of his father's reading materials.

"I guess it is," the woman said.

The first shelf he looked at was full of coffee table books of famous painters. The next shelf had French novels. Down the line were contemporary poetry, gardening, political and law books, anthropology, phycology, and row after row of what seemed to be a random scatter of fiction and nonfiction. There was a reference shelf. He scanned the spines. One was *Living with Diabetes*. He let his finger touch upon it but moved away from the shelf.

"This collection is amazing."

"Thank you."

"How can you keep a bookstore way out here?"

"Mostly for our own use. Though we like the idea of running a bookstore. Which is funny, because we almost never open it. People drive up, see the door shut, and turn around. Happens I heard your feet on the gravel and took a look."

"I'm glad you did. This place is heaven."

"Glad you like it. You a book lover?"

"Yes. For my whole life." In one of the books he found in his father's storage unit, he'd read about books being condemned as "poisonous weeds" during the Cultural Revolution in China and after that, reading took on an immediate sense of illicit knowledge and excitement.

Lewis was eager to talk to this woman. He had been eager to talk to someone in the bar down the road too. "Too much time sitting and reading," he said, and slapped his open palms hard against his gut. There was some truth to that. He'd been a poor eater most of his life. Food as a crutch, he'd been told. He'd been a nervous, then angry kid, and that carried over into adulthood. Anger at his father and then fear to let anyone else close enough to hold such sway over him. He kept from getting close to anyone by staying in constant motion, jumping from ship to ship and ocean to ocean for most of his life. At sea he'd cloistered himself away with books, and recently, since he'd gained his top licensure, with the responsibility of running a ship stressing him out, he started eating junk food.

"Well, you feel free to look around as much as you like. Yell up to the house if I can help you with anything."

"You don't mind leaving me here?"

"Well, it doesn't seem like you can get very far with very much, to be honest, so you're welcome to park it as long as you like."

"Awfully nice of you. Thank you."

"You're welcome." She walked out and left Lewis to wander among the books.

In the back of the room was a yellow sheet for a curtain that he pushed aside and found a low-ceilinged room with no windows. There were white plaster walls, lined with bookshelves of antique, leather-bound books. There was a handwritten journal starting from 1762 of a man named Jacque La Véredrye who was exploring Alberta and living among the native tribes of the plains. He had drawn pictures of the village and faces of the people he lived with. He recorded their day-to-day lives. He wrote about his own life as the son of a French-Canadian trapper who trained him to come to the mountains of the West, but with his immediate fascination with what and who he found on the plains, he wanted to capture the essence of the lives of natives instead of taking anything from the land.

Lewis felt bad that he hadn't kept such a record of his life aboard ships. An active accounting of every thought and feeling from a life adrift. Something like the accumulation of the weekly letters his father had been sending him. There had been times when he'd get back from a long shipping and piles of such letters waited for him. Over the years, Lewis could never bring himself to write back, and the letters asked less and less about Lewis, and became a sharing of his father's inner life. A written path of doubt plowing through one broken man.

Lewis read well into the first volume of the journals in the shed and decided to buy it as a gift for his father. A stand in of at least someone's full accounting of making a way out in the world.

Hours passed. It was exciting to find this spirit laid down on parchment in the middle of an odd and lonely state in the West. After half a day of reading he felt like he had known this author his whole life. As he read this other man's histories he felt something inside of him emerging from a chrysalis. He imagined himself as an early explorer on the Alberta plains, not an isolated man bending toward fat, who had run so far from his family.

He had gotten lost in his father's storage unit books like this as a boy. He wanted to know what his father was looking for in all those pages. At first Lewis found the text dry, too abstract in their arguments and thinking, but his father's margin notes, often written in red marker, often messy to read, were fascinating. There were years of the man's thoughts, his inner life, that Lewis pored over until the payment on the storage unit ran up. Then the books went in his basement where they had water damage, and most were ruined outright or lost to the mold that ensued. All that red ink blurred. His father's thoughts bled away, only to be replaced by his letter writing.

His father's most recent letters came with another round of invitations to his cabin in Montana. His last injury settlement payment was due and he was flying Lewis's brother and sister and their kids out. The letters gave a date of their visit.

His father also wrote, *Please come. If you can't, please tell me where I can come find you. I'll travel anywhere in the world.*

The vulnerability of that last letter made Lewis aware of how he'd hidden so much of his past life away but how it still circled in his head in dark eddies. How he pretended like the past didn't matter. After reading of his father's plea, Lewis had laid his head down and covered his face in his arms to muffle the hot choking sobs. He thought of himself in Montana, face-to-face with his father, of what he would say. He thought of his father leaving when Lewis was a boy. But what can you do about such betrayals. You let them sink all the way into your bones to stay with you forever, and move on.

Lewis did not know how many hours had passed when he heard the woman call out. "Hello. Are you still here?"

"Hi. I'm back here." He started to shuffle to his feet but his legs locked up.

The woman stood in the doorway at the curtain.

"Sorry. I got caught up back here. These books are wonderful."

"The same thing happens to me."

"Can I buy this one?"

"Of course. It will be the first book we've sold all year."

"Great."

"It's getting late, and you're a bit of a way from anywhere."

"That's okay. I'm camping, so I can pull onto a field up ahead."

"You're welcome to camp on our land for the night, if you wish."

"That's kind of you. I'd really appreciate that."

"No problem. I'm Holly."

"Lewis."

"Let me show you around, Lewis."

Lewis was hesitant to put down the Alberta journals of Jacque La Véredrye that he bought.

Holly led him to the back of the house. She pointed to a tall hill to the east.

"The stars are right on top of you back here. You can bring your bike around and use the hill for your campsite."

Lewis retrieved his bike, pitched his bivy sack tent, and changed from his biking clothes to a pair of lightweight shorts, a T-shirt, and sandals. He heated up a package of noodles on his Coleman stove and ate the last of the peanut butter burritos he'd made that morning. He wanted a candy bar. Sugar of any kind. He'd been addicted to it for years, and now he was trying to pedal free of it before it warped his body beyond repair. He was trying to pedal into the past when he was young and healthy and had a family.

When he'd eaten, the sun began to dip in the west. He walked to the house to ask if he could fill his water bottles.

"This must be our wandering bard," a middle-aged blond woman in a green short-sleeved, V-neck jumper said.

"I guess that's me. I spoke with Holly earlier. I'm Lewis."

"Lewis. I'm Katherine, Holly's wife."

"Nice to meet you Katherine. Mind if I fill up my water bottles?"

"Not at all, I can even top the offer of tap water if you'd like to share a glass of wine."

"I'd love that," Lewis said, dismissing the inner critic of his calorie and sugar intake. During his previous shore leave that had been delayed because monsoons made havoc on the ship's itinerary, he stayed in Damascus. There he'd spent his first few days hiding between the sheets in his hotel room from sunup to sundown, bone-tired and only waking with the enchanting calls of the muezzin. Once he was rested, he began taking marathon-length walks around the city, down every dead-end market lane, and using the minarets to keep his bearings. He tried talking to people in the stalls, but buffered by yet another language, he remained isolated and went days without speaking a meaningful word to anyone.

Lewis and Katherine sat in wicker chairs on the veranda of the wraparound porch, each drinking a glass of cold white wine and watching the sunset. Holly came and joined them with her own glass and a new bottle of wine. Her free hand reached out, and she dragged a fingertip across her wife's knuckles. Lewis was drawn to these women, struck right away by their ease with each other, and he envied how they'd made a place for themselves and for having each other.

They talked and drank. The women were both lawyers from Kansas City who wanted to get as far away from the bustle of their careers as they could, and bought the ranch property seven years before and spent their days reveling in their privacy.

"Now I feel bad for butting into your haven," Lewis said.

"I find the wonder you have in our books engaging," Holly said. "Besides, we need some visitors from time to time."

They drank the second bottle and started on a third as it was getting dark. The sky took its time getting dark there.

The women spoke of their lives in Wyoming. They had two extra generators and two meat freezers full of processed elk with select cuts wrapped in brown butcher paper, which helped them get through the bad Chinook storms. They talked of where they came from, their careers.

"What do you do here?" Lewis asked.

"We paint," Katherine said.

"What do you do when you're not painting?"

"Talk about painting," Holly jumped in.

Then Lewis began asking about the books and how they came upon the leather-bound frontier journals.

"Nothing special, I'm afraid," Holly said. "An estate sale in Jackson Hole. Not sure where they traveled before that. Not really sure if they're worth more than you paid or not."

They kept talking and drinking wine, and it seemed his hosts were as eager for the company as he was. They asked about his bike route, the logistics, and if he'd taken other trips like this.

He hadn't. This was a once-in-a-lifetime trip. It seemed important to take.

They told him of trips they'd taken. "We went this last spring to Kearny, Nebraska, to see the sand hill cranes migrate," Holly said.

"That is a sight," Katherine agreed, "but it happens when the weather is awful."

"We drove down there and before the sun came up went to sit in a lean-to to watch them by the river," Holly said.

"They dance with each other," Katherine said.

"How so?" Lewis asked.

"Well, it's hard to describe," Holly said. She pushed back her chair and started moving around in a circle, as an auger digging through the deck until she was coiled with bent knees. She sprung upward, leaped off the ground higher than he would have guessed her age would allow, her arms shot outward, fingers fanned out, knuckles taut, and for a minute she was frozen in midjump. Levitating. She landed and jumped again, as if never touching the deck. Her neck, delicate and white, elongated, and her ponytail swayed from shoulder to shoulder.

"And they sing," Katherine said.

"How do they sing?"

Holly kept jumping.

Katherine started making birdsongs that sounded like a piercing wind pushing through a canyon.

Even as it was happening, Lewis knew he would remember these two women dancing and doing birdcalls for the rest of his days. Watching them he felt the troll of his own loneliness that clung to his back and kept him beneath the currents of being with and loving others.

When they said good night, Lewis walked out to the field to his tent. He leaped and spun several times, imitating Holly imitating a crane. He was happy and full of energy despite his sore legs and rear. He was happy to have found Jacque La Véredrye and what that man had laid down in those pages. He felt the flicker of youthful love of the wider world that he had burned with as a young man.

Instead of going to sleep, he took a flashlight and wandered farther up the hill in order to get even closer to the white pulse and heartbeat of the stars as they came out. When he reached the boulders, he climbed over a few and came to the top of the rise. There he looked east and saw what looked like a string of stars resting on the ground. A runway to the past. When he focused his eyes, he realized they were a long line of lantern lights. There must have been hundreds of people walking across the nowhere landscape toward the hill he stood on. Lewis stood watching for a minute, unsure if he was drunker than he thought or if the fun-house mirror in Natrona had blurred his vision. He climbed down the rocks and ran across the field back to the deck where Katherine and Holly were holding hands and sipping wine.

"Maybe I'm going crazy, but it looks like a thousand people are hiking up to your property over that hill."

"Mormons," Holly said. "You know how I told you we moved to the middle of nowhere to get away from people, especially judgmental people? Well, we didn't think to ask if this ranch was smack on the Mormon Trail."

"You're kidding?"

"Nope. Every summer, thousands of them come marching along. That's why we've got all those posted signs on our fence."

"They're going to Utah. Mormon pilgrims by the millions. An endless procession of them. They come bearing down on us and then loop around, because we put up such a stink, and they didn't want to deal directly with a pair of pussy-bearing, pussy-loving lawyers."

"That's the damnedest thing."

"You're telling us," Holly said.

Lewis walked back to his tent, climbed the hill again, and looked down on the Mormon pilgrims. He lit his Zippo and let it burn in front of him. He hoped the people far below would see the flicker of light as he licked his finger and passed it through the flame, over and over, as if sending a signal. It was clear to him then that every hidden corner of the country was too complex to really understand. People shift from one place to another too fast, coming and going from everywhere. The whole country seemed to offer up people made to feel small by one thing or another. Sun. Space. Each other. Tiny Americans everywhere. Drifting and drifting.

But God, he loved the West. The air, the land changing from stark to beautiful along every line on a map, and the endless versions of people filling their days. He loved how he could reinvent himself a little every day. He would break camp early in the morning and bike on toward Montana to make it by the date his father had given him. His father's cabin in the mountains now felt every bit as important as the destination the pilgrims in the valley below sought. In the morning, he would get on his bike and go forth as a man who opens his heart to the world.

14

Terrance Thurber, 2018

The entire visit was a reckoning Terrance had been inviting for most of his life. As the date drew closer, it felt like a lifetime of his being one sort of person, then slowly turning into another kind of person, again and again, was about to crest upon him and reveal who he really was. He had not been able to sleep well for most of the week. Helen would wake and find him either restless on the couch, at his desk writing letters to Lewis, or out on the deck, taking in the cold air and all the stars over the valley. She'd sit with him until he'd either try to go back to bed or the sun came up and he'd go out into the woods to start his day.

"I keep thinking of my kids following me into the trees," he said.

"I think they'll really like it here," Helen said.

"I do too." He knocked one boot against the other to loosen dried dirt but didn't step off the deck.

"They will," she said.

Terrance and Helen picked up Jamie and Tina, and Connor and Dennis, from the airport early that morning. As soon as they came out of the security gate, he felt how years of imagining their lives had been weighing on him deep in his body. He could hardly move and felt dangerously exposed as they walked closer.

"Welcome," Helen called out, and held open her arms, as if to take them all in.

Terrance cupped his hands around Jamie's face. "There's my girl," he said, but his chest tightened and he fell silent.

He turned to greet Tina and Dennis.

"You have the same eyebrows," Helen said as Terrance and Connor stood together after giving each other a brief handshake.

Terrance looked at the choked expression reddening his son's face and recognized the continuation of the softer half of his own nature. It was so obvious it made him uneasy, like he'd just felt the earth's slow, imperceptible motion.

When they'd gathered their luggage, he drove them all back to the cabin in the van he rented for the week. Closer to his cabin they drove by a fruit stand where Buddy, a bull-chested mastiff dog, slept under the produce tables. Then they passed the Pine Bark café, which he imagined taking them to later in the week for cheeseburgers and strawberry pie.

Now he was trying to busy himself making them lunch. Trying to do one small task at a time and let them warm up to him. To seeing him again. To how old he must seem to them. He wanted to give them space to begin to say and feel whatever they needed to. Seeing them now, he could barely contain himself from pulling them closer and hugging them all. He also imagined falling onto his knees and begging for their forgiveness.

Helen had given them warm hugs at the airport and kept

them talking, offering spaces for Terrance to jump into their conversations all morning. Helen settled them into the rooms they would stay in for the week. She placed a hand on Terrance's arm. He was slicing a loaf of sandwich bread he'd baked outside in the stone oven.

"You're doing great," she said. He stared at the cracked skin on his knuckles and his thumb that was purple from an errant hammer strike.

"Thanks, love."

Helen made tea and they all sat around the dining room talking, but their voices stilled as he came back in. He placed the bread next to a plate of meats, cheeses, spreads, and a large salad he'd made that morning. Terrance sensed he had interrupted Jamie and Connor's catching up.

Tina lifted and dipped the string of her teabag. Jamie cupped the steaming mug in her palms and blew on it. He was eager to take them outside and show them his narrow valley, the eddies in the river with the most beautiful speckled trout, and the un-hindered view from high up the mountainside.

"Eat. Please. Eat," he said.

Tina and Dennis started making themselves sandwiches. Fresh-picked mountain flowers arranged in jelly jars lined the window behind them.

"You know, I'd be tempted to lose a testicle if it meant I got to retire and live in this place," Dennis teased.

Connor took a jab at his son's shoulder but was grinning, clearly sharing the same sense of humor as his son.

"I didn't lose it," Terrance said. "Can you imagine what I

could have gotten if I had though? We could have done this little family reunion on a giant yacht. Hired your Uncle Lewis to captain it for us."

"Do you know that it was because of Mom that Lewis went into the navy?" Jamie jumped in. Her face reddened immediately, embarrassed to have brought up their mother so soon.

"How so?" Terrance asked.

"Remember when Lewis took that bus trip out here and ended up staying at that girls' camp? He had the paperwork for all four branches of the military in his bag. Mom dug around for them and took them out in the bus station when he went to the bathroom. She thought she grabbed them all but guess which one she missed."

"Come on," Connor said.

"True story."

"I was in the room with him when he packed his bag," Connor said. "He put that navy application in with his college folders. I think he meant to toss the whole thing in the trash and pick from the others. I thought for sure he'd pick the marines."

"Do you even remember Mom?" Jamie blurted out, then looked down into her lap. "I'm sorry."

"Don't be." Terrance stayed silent then. Waiting. He wanted this from her, from all of them.

"So, what is going on with Mom?" Connor asked.

Terrance could sense that old nervousness in Connor, the family peacemaker, always racing ahead to where he sensed trouble, trying to distract everyone from a collision.

Jamie looked over at Tina. Smiled at her, as if smoothing over the feeling that made her take a shot at her father. "Did you know she's in South Carolina now? Tina and I went down there a few times to visit."

"Yeah," Connor said.

"She's doing well too. She keeps busy. Paints the dunes and waves and sells her stuff to tourist shops." She laughed a bit and looked at Terrance. "You guys could have started a business like that together."

"Bones and Beaches," Terrance said.

"Yeah," Jamie gave a tense laugh. "You two would have made a killing." She dabbed at the corner of her eye before she went on. "The first time we went to visit, Tina was only ten. Do you remember that trip?"

"Of course. The turtles," Tina said.

"Turtles?" Connor asked.

"Mom volunteers for this group. What's it called, Tina?"

"NEST. Network for Endangered Sea Turtles. They monitor the nests."

"Good memory. Yeah, so we're down there, and she comes into our room in the middle of the night. Whispers to us and asks, 'Do you want to be the moon?'"

"Oh boy," Connor said.

"No. Not like that. She's not like that anymore. She'd gotten a call from this NEST group. They have these loggerhead sea turtles down there that leave their eggs buried in the sand. On nights when the eggs hatch and there's no moon out, the baby sea turtles go toward the nearby streetlights and never find the ocean."

"It was so cool," Tina jumped in. "There were almost a dozen nests with little turtles digging their way out of the sand. We were given flashlights and told to stand in the surf in front of our assigned turtle nests with the lights over our heads."

"Tina had to pin herself against me to stay sturdy against the surf. I was so afraid she'd get pulled out."

"No. You were afraid of sharks," Tina said. "But I loved it."

"I know. You kept yelling, 'Grandma, Grandma, I can feel them brushing up against my legs.'"

It was the first time Terrance had heard one of his grandkids refer to anyone as their grandparent. Helen reached under the table and held his hand. Tina excused herself and went to the back of the cabin. She was already a grown woman. A childhood behind her already. He kept quiet. He waited to hear what other stories they might want to tell him about the scattered factions of his old life.

Though he already knew all about the South Carolina condo. He'd paid for that with the first batch of his injury money.

What Jamie and Connor didn't know was that Catrin had gotten into a minor car wreck after the kids were grown and out of the house. She put the car in a ditch and dislocated her left hip. She had a short stay in the hospital, which kept her from having to stay a few days in jail. There was to be a court date for a DWI. A mess of money needed. She called Terrance for the first time in years. She wanted to know what to do, not wanting to burden the kids.

"I can't do this," Catrin said. "The kids are all gone. I have nothing here."

It was then they talked for the first time in years. He listened to her spill a decade of worry and pain. When he hung up he told Helen everything he was feeling. How hearing Catrin had brought up the memories of his greatest sins, which were still living, pulsing entities that shadowed him. He imagined his old house and all those painful memories. But then there was the memory of himself as a younger man too. As a new dad. The pace of life was staggering. He remembered holding all the babies in this house. Each as infants crying all night like machines. Toothaches, diapers, and wet beds. It felt like years without sleeping and stress becoming a solid sludge between him and Catrin. He saw how strained and human they had been and felt the ache of it.

It was Helen's suggestion that they help her. Helen believed that helping Catrin would relieve some of the guilt he felt for leaving Catrin and the kids those many, many years ago.

Terrance called Catrin back the next morning and agreed to help her sell the house and move away, a break as far and drastic as the one he had made.

"So what sort of itinerary do you have lined up for us?" Jamie asked, breaking him from his reverie.

"Two fifteen: chop wood. Two thirty: hunt bear," Connor teased.

Terrance laughed at the joke, but he had been dreaming of this day for years. He desperately wanted to show them the breath of his valley. The fog in the morning. The stars a blur of milk-colored light at night. He wanted them to come to know him through all manner of his current home in hopes they'd sense how deeply he wanted to know them.

Terrance looked at his two grown children and asked himself, *Who were they, those beautiful children who used to look up to me? Did they see how much I loved them? Did that break through to them despite me going away?* Looking back, there is Connor walking around with a finger dipped in red paint, waggling it in front of him after he saw *E.T.* There is thin-armed Lewis in the backyard whipping a length of rope at empty cans he hung from the trees like Indiana Jones. There is Jamie flinging herself around the living room pretending to be Mary Lou Retton or sprinting around the house like Flo-Jo.

Terrance could still hear their young voices. They all came running into the house after school, talking over one another, their need and desire to share themselves a flash flood pushing off the daytime silence. One day they came home in shock after their whole school watched the launch of the *Challenger*—the hope and awe of learning about teachers going up into space before the fiery, confusing end. There was Jamie, who horrified Terrance by walking into the house singing "Like a Virgin," before he'd ever heard of Madonna. There was teeth-chattering Jamie standing over the heating vent to get warm, the hem of her sweater held out to catch the air. And here is Jamie now. This grown woman and mother and beneath all that years of unasked and unanswered questions. Terrance was ready and waiting to receive them now.

When they finished eating, Helen kissed Terrance on the top of the head. "I'll clean up. Why don't you go show everyone the woods."

"Great idea," Jamie said. "Some fresh air would be nice."

"I'd love that," Terrance said. He got up and went to the bathroom before they left. When he opened the door he saw his reflection in the opened medicine cabinet mirror, and heard the rattle of Tina shoving a pill bottle back inside.

"Sorry. Sorry. Not used to company I guess," Terrance said, shutting the door.

He stood in the hallway stunned. If she was snooping he hoped she was still too young to know what Helen's pills really meant. If she was stealing, he wanted to tell her how sad that made him. He wanted to square her shoulders to the mirror and tell her to look at all the versions of herself she could become. He wanted to tell her there was no promise the world will catch you as often as it lets you fall. He felt the need to confront her, but he didn't even know her. And it was too soon to have anything like that come up. He turned from the door and knew he would keep what he'd seen to himself. It made him dizzy how ingrained secrets were in his nature, or maybe even the nature of all social creatures.

Out in the foyer Helen pointed at the stack of shoes, and mock clapped at the pile of people in the home. She was beside herself with joy to have everyone there. He reached out and took her hand and pressed her palm against his cheek.

When they were all ready to go, they trekked out onto the deck, down the steps, and into the opening where he led them into the forest. Halfway across the field, when he could already hear the river, he stopped talking so they would sense it themselves.

When they stepped into the woods and could hear the distant push of the river, Tina and Dennis hurried ahead. Magpies sprung from the hemlock trees.

When Terrance and his two children caught up, Tina stepped a pale white foot into the water, then pulled it out. Cold enough to shock the system even at the height of summer. She got on her hands and knees on the bank. A rivulet of clear mountain water ran between two smoothed obsidian stones and now flowed over his granddaughter's hands. She made a cup with her palms, the pinkies close as slow dancers, the stack of fingers curved upward and wanting. She brought the water up to splash her face, and made an exasperated *auuugh* sound that peeled off into a quick, happy laugh.

"There's something else to show you," Terrance said.

They followed him away from the river and deeper into the trees.

Jamie draped an arm over Tina's shoulders. "Every one of these trees has a heartbeat. Right, Dad?"

"That's right," Terrance said.

"What is that?" Connor asked, and pointed to the clearing.

They silently walked into the open space with the giant bone creature.

Terrance stayed back and watched them walk up to and around the bone sculpture, now weathered and twice rebuilt from the wear of snow and winds. The polished bones glistened like coral.

He watched them each take turns reaching out to touch the creature and was overcome with having them here. He had dreamed of such a moment so fiercely that now it felt like a prayer coming true before his eyes.

"Did you make this?" Jamie asked.

"Yes."

"This is amazing," Connor said.

"It is," Dennis said.

Terrance felt his heart tense and found it hard to talk.

Connor was crouched by the foreleg gently running a hand over the base. Dennis and Tina both walked backward to take in the scale of the sculpture. Jamie slowly walked another circle around the statue. "You could put this in a show."

"This was my first."

"There are more?" she asked.

Terrance waved them to follow, and turning up the hillside, led them to the next, and then the next sculpture. The valley was a sculpture park now from years of his daily efforts. A herd of strange creatures run off from his imagination and frozen mid-stride, midlife.

One of the largest sculptures reared upright, antlers as hands reaching for the canopy above. Helen had wanted him to take pictures of what he had done and send them to the kids, but he never would. He wanted this. For them to see. For them to be here. For him to show them something he had done with his time.

Dennis made talons of his hands and held them over his head to pose for a picture next to the sculpture.

They spent most of the afternoon hiking from creature to creature. He kept stealing glances at all of them, making room for their visages to imprint upon his mind. Back in Olean, when he felt himself spiraling, there was that one selfish thought that grew so big it split him at the core. *You get no more of me*, some voice deep in him said. It was this thought, that he mattered most, should come first, that made his exit possible. This was also the thought that cleared space for him to get sober and heal from old pains, but which left a chasm for grief and the specter of his children to fill in. Now, he knew there was no getting out of life clean, and if they asked, he'd give his children anything. All his money, time, property, and attention. Now he knew everyone must do this in some form or another. Only with the surprise of that, which came to him when Helen came along, and now again with these adult-children-strangers-flesh-and-blood, did he feel how sweet life could become.

He led them back to the cabin to rest and to make them dinner. On the walk home, he picked harsh blackberries and wild rhubarb he'd boil together with sugar and pour over ice cream for their dessert.

Dennis wanted to see the barn with all the tools. Everyone else went back to the cabin.

"We can go look for antlers in the morning," Terrance said.

"Can we make something like you did out of them?" Dennis asked.

"Sure." He led Dennis to a ladder on the side of the barn near the compost heap. "Have a look up there."

Dennis climbed up high enough he could see how the roof was covered with elk horns and other bones drying in the sun.

"There are so many."

"Sometimes I saw the smaller antlers into six-inch lengths to sell to a local store for dog chews. Makes easy money. Gives me something to do."

Inside the barn Dennis almost knocked over the bucket in the middle of the floor. He bent down to look closer inside of it, not sure what he was really looking at. It was half full of water and floating mice.

"What is this?"

Terrance walked closer and gave the bucket a tap with the toe of his boot.

"It's effective." There were two notches in the rim of the bucket where he laid a length of a smooth steel rod across the mouth. "Put a bit of peanut butter in the center and cover the pole with Vaseline. They can't resist and slip right in."

"They drown?"

"Yep. Keeps them from eating my horns." Terrance looked at the slick crosswalk over the bucket and imagined a tiny version of himself on such a slick path, then he saw tiny versions of his family following right behind him.

"Do you leave them here?" Dennis asked.

"They're not going anywhere."

Terrance showed his grandson all the tools in his workspace. He looked at it anew with the realization Dennis was the only person other than Helen and the men who constructed the barn to have ever seen the inside of it. He saw his own footprints stamped into the bone dust and the racks of plaster of paris, papier-mâché, and hardware he'd used to bind the bones.

He looked at Dennis then and thought, *If we both close our eyes at the same time and sit still we will hear the same blood pumping.*

When he finished showing off his tools, Terrance and Dennis walked closer to the cabin.

Terrance pointed to a shaded brown bird with a bright yellow nape hopping on the ground. "That's a horned lark. I don't see those too often."

On the porch, Helen was on the rocking swing with Tina. The two of them were so close their shoulders were touching, leaning into each other like old confidants. Something caught his eye up the road.

A bike glided down the driveway.

The rider wore a neon-green jersey and red helmet. Terrance watched the bike get closer.

The tires wobbled over the gravel and lifted up a chalky plume of dirt. The rider broke into a clearing of full sun and his whole body reflected the light. Terrance had to shield his eyes from the glow until the rider was close enough to make out his face—a little tired, handsomeness tinged by time or grief.

"Oh please," Terrance gasped. "Please," and a feeling of inner expansiveness that began with his family in the woods swelled again and engulfed him as this rider slowed to a stop in front of him. He felt the enormity of the moment as the rider cut through the blinding light and the vision felt like a reward for enduring everything he'd been given.

"Oh please, be you. Oh please be you," he said as the rider damp with sweat and with bright clothes that glowed took him into his arms.

"Hi, Dad. It took me a while to find the place."

Terrance bent into Lewis's arms and knew he would end-lessly re-create this day in his mind, and that the effort would take the memory of all his days to do it justice.

Acknowledgments

This book is the product of years of labor guided by many loving hands.

Special thanks to my remarkable agent, Rayhané Sanders, and editors, Laura Brown and Hannah Robinson, who lovingly coaxed forward the story of this complicated family.

Eternal thanks to everyone at Harper Perennial who made this book happen and to Erica Ferguson for helping get it all right.

For their guidance I owe a deep debt to Steven Schwartz, Jonis Agee, Jonathan Starke, and all my friends and colleges at St. Bonaventure University, Colorado State University, University of Nebraska–Lincoln, and Bradley University and all points in between.

Great and growing love to my family, especially my parents, Tony and Mariette Murphy, for their constant love and support. Hyat, Nora, and Jude, you fill my life with your joy, energy, and love. I am so grateful I get to watch you enter our odd and lovely world.

To Becca, so often I turn around and am shocked by your glowing presence and how much I love you. This one is for you. They all are.

About the Author

Devin Murphy is the nationally bestselling author of *The Boat Runner*. His fiction has appeared in more than sixty literary journals and anthologies, including the *Missouri Review, Glimmer Train,* and *Confrontation*. He is an associate professor at Bradley University and lives in Chicago with his wife and kids.

www.devinmurphyauthor.com

ALSO BY
DEVIN MURPHY

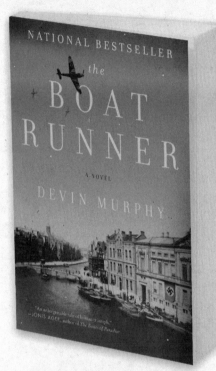

THE BOAT RUNNER
A NOVEL
AVAILABLE IN PAPERBACK, EBOOK, AND DIGITAL AUDIO

"Chilling . . . deadly earnest . . . full of discomfiting nuance . . . an astute and riveting portrait of one young man." —*New York Times Book Review*

Epic in scope and featuring a thrilling narrative with precise, elegant language, *The Boat Runner* tells the little-known story of the young Dutch boys who were thrown into the Nazi campaign, as well as the brave boatmen who risked everything to give Jewish refugees safe passage to land abroad. Through one boy's harrowing tale of personal redemption, here is a novel about the power of people's stories and voices to shine light through our darkest days, until only love prevails.